Praise for Richard T. Ryan's Sherlock Holmes Adventures

The Vatican Cameos

Winner of the Underground Book Reviews' "Novel of the Year" Award. Winner Silver Medal in the Readers' Favorite book-award contest.

"[*The Vatican Cameos* is] an extravagantly imagined and beautifully written Holmes story." – Lee Child, NY Times Bestselling author and the creator of Jack Reacher

"*The Vatican Cameos* opens with a familiar feel for fans of Arthur Conan Doyle's original Sherlock Holmes stories. The plotting is clever, and the alternating stories well-told." – Crime Thriller Hound

The Stone of Destiny

"Sometimes a book comes along that absolutely restores your faith in reading. Such is the 'found manuscript' of Dr. Watson, *The Stone of Destiny*. Exhilarating, superb narrative and a cast of characters that are as dark as they are vivid. ... A thriller of the very first rank." – Ken Bruen, author of *The Guards, The Magdalen Martyrs,* and many other novels, as well as the creator of the Jack Taylor series

"Somewhere Sir Arthur Conan Doyle is smiling. Ryan's *The Stone of Destiny* is a fine addition to the Canon." – Reed Farrel Coleman, NY Times Bestselling author of *What You Break*

"Richard Ryan's prose flows as easily as a stream in the summer. I thought the way the Stone was stolen, how it was transported out of England under the very noses of the army of police, and its hiding place in Ireland were brilliant!" – Raven Reviews

The Druid of Death

"The clever solution, which echoes one from a golden age classic, is the book's best feature." – Publishers Weekly

"… the Druidic detail and the depiction of 19th-century London are fascinating and delightful." – Kirkus Reviews

"As one would expect from a Sherlock Holmes story, the Great Detective's intellect, keen eye for observation, and logical deductions all play a factor in the satisfying conclusion of this mystery." – Kristopher Zgorski, founder of BOLO Books

The Merchant of Menace

Short-listed for the annual Drunken Druid Award.

"Oh, what a joy it is to meet Sherlock Holmes and Dr. Watson again! *The Merchant of Menace* is an exciting adventure of priceless valuables, great detective work and just the kind of devilish adversary we love to read about." – Mattias Boström, author of *From Holmes to Sherlock: The Story of the Men and Women Who Created an Icon*

"This rousing, intriguing, devilishly fun caper, well-executed and well-paced, had me hooked from the first page. The dutiful Watson, Holmes' deductive skills, and a worthy nemesis to rival the evil Moriarty himself, make this cat-and-mouse adventure a page-turning, edge-of-your-seat roller-coaster ride well worth taking." – Tracy Clark, author of *Broken Places* and *Borrowed Time* and the creator of Cass Raines

"With an intriguing premise and a cunning plot, *The Merchant of Menace* will delight Sherlockians of all stripes. Richard T. Ryan has given us a gripping mystery and a loving tribute to the Great Detective." – Daniel Stashower, author of *Teller of Tales: The Life of Arthur Conan Doyle*

Through a Glass Starkly

"Deftly blending Conan Doyle and Dan Brown, Richard Ryan's *Through a Glass Starkly* offers an intriguing mix of history and mystery. Remaining true to the Canon in his depictions of the iconic Holmes and Watson, Ryan also delivers a mystery that should satisfy even the most demanding Sherlockian." – Robert Dugoni, NY Times Bestselling author of *The Eighth Sister* and the creator of Tracy Crosswhite

"Ryan's Watsonian voice is superb, and as with his earlier novels the author has included several affectionate nods to the characters, stories, and intrigues of the original Canon. These twists and turns make this an engrossing and enjoyable read, as do the variety of colourful locations chosen for the action. From a secret *pied-a-terre* in Paris, to the Whispering Gallery in St. Paul's Cathedral, we are carried along at a frenetic pace. I previously read, and thoroughly enjoyed, *The Druid of Death*. *Through a Glass Starkly* is even better!" – Sherlock Holmes Society of London

"Another brilliant addition to the Sherlock Holmes Canon." – Bruce Robert Coffin, author of the Detective Byron mysteries

Three May Keep a Secret

"Richard T. Ryan's *Three May Keep a Secret* [is] a pitch-perfect adventure that pits Conan Doyle's great detective against a master criminal...It's a tale of fabulous jewels, brilliant forgeries, cunning disguises and a Watson double-act that will make every writer who's ever penned a Holmes pastiche green with 'Why didn't I think of that?'" – Jeffrey Hatcher, screenwriter for *Mr. Holmes*

"... the book's strengths, including the imaginative setup, make Ryan's taking up Conan Doyle's mantle again welcome. Fans of traditional pastiches will enjoy this." – Publishers Weekly

"The tour de force in the book is the presence of a criminal mastermind, a worthy replacement for Professor Moriarty, whose shadows are broodingly present in the adventure." – *Sherlock Holmes Society of India*

The Poisoned Pawn

"Richard Ryan has again penned another fast paced and carefully plotted pastiche. The characterizations are both strong and canonical. The story is replete with the requisite twists and turns, intriguing villains, and surprise endings. It moves quickly, establishes the necessary atmosphere, and maintains the quality that he's long developed." – Robert Katz, MD, BSI

"An absorbing narrative with a devilish plot – top marks for Richard T. Ryan's latest novel which captures the true spirit of Conan Doyle." – Mark Mower, author of *Sherlock Holmes: The Baker Street Archive*

"It's indeed a pleasure to read a novel in which Professor Moriarty is pulling the strings of another criminal from behind the scenes. In *The Poisoned Pawn*, Richard T. Ryan has the professor maneuver a villain seeking personal revenge into a deadly game against Sherlock Holmes. A rousing adventure from start to finish!" — Ray Riethmeier, editor of *Sherlock Holmes: Stranger Than Truth* and *Sherlock Holmes: Stranger Than Fiction*

The Devil's Disciples

"Richard T. Ryan has done it again! Holmes and Watson go undercover in their quest to thwart the nefarious deeds of a group of terrorists. The result is as riveting as it is clever. If you like a great Sherlock Holmes story, you'll love *The Devil's Disciples*!" – Jack Sacco, author of the Pulitzer Prize nominated *Where the Birds Never Sing*

"Richard Ryan has a flair for bringing history to life. This book gives a balanced, sensitive view of the Irish-British conflicts in the 1880s. He has Holmes and Watson take the reader through 19th-century London from the Tower of London and Westminster Abby to the depths of a Whitechapel pub. It is a very worthwhile piece of historical fiction." – Charles Blanksteen, BSI

"Ryan understands the time period, the events and the critical historic characters. He also understands Watson and Holmes. He does an excellent job of intertwining the two; fact and fiction. It's not just a mystery, it is an adventure with 19th-century terrorists. Or are they?" – Kieran E. McMullen, Sherlockian author whole titles include *Sherlock Holmes and the Irish Rebels*

The Traitorous Templars

"It's the story Conan Doyle should have thought of!" – Burt Wolder, BSI, co-host of the I Hear of Sherlock Everywhere (IHOSE) podcast

"This adventure is a fascinating case with Holmes at his best, and one is left wondering what Ryan will share with us next time." – David Marcum, Sherlockian scholar and editor

"Richard Ryan's prodigious historical research shines through in The Traitorous Templar, but he never hits you over the head with it to impress you." – Paul Singleton, BSI

The Other Woman:
A Sherlock Holmes Adventure

by Richard T. Ryan

Hardcover ISBN 978-1-80424-723-5
Paperback ISBN 978-1-80424-724-2
ePub 978-1-80424-725-9
PDF 978-1-80424-726-6

Published by MX Publishing
335 Princess Park Manor, Royal Drive, London, N11 3GX
www.mxpublishing.co.uk

Cover design by Brian Belanger

For Brody, Henry and Riley and

of course, my wife, Grace

Foreword

Several years ago, while I was visiting my brother in Scotland, I placed what turned out to be the winning bid on a locked chest at an estate auction in the town of St. Andrews. I had no idea what the contents might be, so I truly was buying a pig in a poke.

Readers familiar with my work since then are aware that inside the chest I discovered a battered tin dispatch box filled with unpublished manuscripts written by Dr. John Watson, whose name had been stenciled on the outside.

To this day, I still have no idea whether the tin box I acquired is the one mentioned by Watson in "The Problem of Thor Bridge" and other stories in the Canon or another one entirely. As fans of the Great Detective are well aware, Watson was under the impression that his box was locked away safe inside the vault of Cox & Co. in Charing Cross.

Given everything I have extracted from the box in my possession and read thus far, I'm inclined to think Dr. Watson must have secreted at least two boxes of untold or unpublished tales and possibly more. One reason I say this is because I have to date encountered only one of the more than one hundred untold tales to which the good doctor alludes throughout the Canon in the box in my possession. Then again, I still have a large number of manuscripts clamoring for my attention.

As I have indicated in the past, some tales appear to have been held back for political reasons; others were not published out of a sense of Victorian propriety; still others failed to see the light of day because of explicit instructions issued by one or both of the Holmes brothers. Finally, I have come to believe that two or three additional cases wounded Holmes's vanity in some way and thus were destined for eternal obscurity.

After you have read this particular adventure, I think you will see that it failed to find its way to a publisher's desk for several different reasons – one or two of which you might not expect.

I also believe this particular tale also illustrates an aspect of Holmes's personality with which we are familiar – I'll leave it to you to figure out what that is – but in this instance we are afforded a particularly nuanced version of the Great Detective. In all honesty, after my first reading of this manuscript, I had some qualms about bringing it to print. I struggled with myself, playing devil's advocate as I argued back and forth, until I finally determined that the public deserved to see this tale and decide for themselves. I feel enough time has passed, and sensibilities have changed.

Fans of Holmes can certainly make up their own minds.

Therefore, although I still harbor more than a few misgivings, I will let the readers decide for themselves.

So, gentle reader, I have attempted, admittedly in a rather vague fashion, to give you fair warning. To underscore that point, I should like to quote no less a personage than Geoffrey Chaucer, who is often hailed as the father of English literature.

Chaucer looked at life and detailed what he saw – warts and all. However, he also went to great pains to take his readers' tastes and sensibilities into account. At the beginning of "The Miller's Tale," a fairly ribald story, he maintains that he must use truth as his guide. In other words, Chaucer felt compelled to tell it like it is.

With regard to this particular adventure, I am of a like mind. So like Chaucer, I would humbly suggest that if you feel this tale is going to offend you, stop right here, replace the book on the shelf, and to use Chaucer's words:

Turne over the leef and chese another tale.

– *Richard T. Ryan*
March, 14, 2025

Introduction

Throughout his long and illustrious career, Sherlock Holmes found himself matching wits with an amazing array of ne'er-do-wells from thieves and counterfeiters, to blackmailers and murderers. Like his clients, his adversaries came from every rung of the social ladder.

While many people would regard his vanquishing of Professor Moriarty at the Reichenbach Falls to be the pinnacle of his career – and it certainly was at that time – I would humbly suggest that his accomplishments in resolving this particular adventure, which I have chosen to title *The Other Woman; A Sherlock Holmes Adventure,* are on a par with those efforts of his which I have detailed in "The Final Problem" and "The Empty House."

I say that because while Professor Moriarty was indeed a criminal mastermind, fully deserving of the title Holmes bestowed on him – "the Napoleon of crime" – much of Moriarty's focus centered on enriching himself and to a lesser degree his faithful followers. He was at once brilliant and ruthless, but his ambition was also limited, if you will, by his rather shortsighted worldview.

Holmes's adversary in this case had adopted a much broader *weltanschauung,* to use the current German equivalent, now so in vogue. A practitioner of *realpolitik* – and obviously a student of Machiavelli's *The Prince* – he would have inflicted death on hundreds of thousands of innocent souls and untold suffering on tens of millions more. This case pushed Holmes to his limits and showed my friend's brilliance in a hitherto unseen way.

As you might suspect, there was an immediacy about this case which made it imperative Holmes tax himself and bring all his powers to bear on a solution. One must also never lose sight of the fact that the stakes were enormous. The slightest misstep on Holmes's part might well have ended in tragedy and chaos and resulted in a much different world order than the one with which we are familiar. Fortunately, Holmes discerned a path forward where others might have simply thrown up their hands in exasperation.

In short, I have never been more proud of my friend than I was when this case was concluded.

As had happened on occasion, I was strictly forbidden to release any of the details surrounding this case to the general public by no less a figure than Mycroft Holmes himself. His warning was stern and to the point, and although he said nothing specific, his manner suggested dire consequences could befall me should I defy his prohibition.

However, I felt that my friend's exertions deserved to be chronicled, and while I believed – and still maintain he should have been recognized in some formal way for his accomplishments – others, more highly placed, apparently took a decidedly different view of things.

Despite their threats and warnings, I have determined to commit this case to paper, knowing full well that no one besides myself may ever read it. I understand the rationale behind the interdiction, yet I remain optimistic that at some point in the far distant future, someone may stumble across my efforts, read what I have written, and agree with me that in many ways this was Sherlock Holmes's finest moment.

– Doctor John Watson
11 October, 1902

Postscriptum – From time to time, I revisit the tales that have never been published. I read them and wonder what changes I might make that would allow them to pass muster with either Holmes or his brother. To be honest, I am not one who looks at his work through rose-coloured glasses or with an overly critical eye. I mention this because of all the untold tales to which I have alluded and many of which I have secretly chronicled, this remains among my favourites and one that I hope sees the light of day someday – not for myself but because I truly believe this was Holmes at his absolute best.

16 July, 1907

What improves the circumstances of the greater part can never be regarded as an inconveniency to the whole. No society can surely be flourishing and happy, of which the far greater part of the members are poor and miserable.

– Adam Smith
Wealth of Nations

There are a thousand hacking at the branches of evil
to one who is striking at the root.

– Henry David Thoreau

Revenge is an act of passion; vengeance of justice.
Injuries are revenged; crimes are avenged.

– Dr. Samuel Johnson

Chapter One – July 1902

Sherlock Holmes returned early one evening in late July, and upon entering our flat and seeing me in my chair, stated, "Watson, I have just had a most singular experience."

For anything to make such an impression upon Holmes was indeed unusual. "Do tell, old man," I encouraged him.

"I had just emerged from my bolt hole in the Shadwell section of the East End where I had followed one of the suspects in the recent theft of the Gough Map from the Bodleian Library. As I am sure you know, the Gough Map, one of the earliest maps of Britain, is a national treasure and as such is priceless."

Actually, I was unaware of the existence of the Gough Map, let alone its worth, but I always hated confessing my ignorance to Holmes, so I replied, "Really, I hadn't heard anything about it."

"I should hope not. The university trustees have spent a great deal of money to cover up the theft, and rather than involve the police, they have tasked me with recovering the map as well as the other stolen documents. In the meantime, at my suggestion, they are updating their security measures throughout the various buildings."

"I don't understand. If the theft occurred in Oxford, why are you following a man here in London?"

"Because I am certain he was involved, if not the mastermind. Everett Majors is no ordinary thief. After attending the Royal Military College at Sandhurst, he spent several years in the army serving with distinction in Ireland with the 1st Dragoons. However, like so many others he found the lure of easy money too tempting to resist and resigned his commission before scandal overtook him.

"As a result of his training, he is a master planner. Were Professor Moriarty still alive, I am certain he would have taken Majors in hand and honed and developed his skills even further. However, I digress. Upon learning where Majors was living after his arrival in London, I set a team of my Irregulars to watch him. Today, I decided to check on him myself. After several frustrating hours during which he never left his rooms, I elected to doff my disguise, change into my frock coat and collar, and return here to pass the time in more pleasant surroundings. The lads have been instructed to notify me immediately should Majors receive any visitors or leave his flat, and they are to follow him if he does.

"At any rate, as I boarded an omnibus, I noticed a young man clamber aboard at the last minute. He was not too tall, slightly built and wearing a rather distinctive double-breasted waistcoat and a wheel cap that seemed incongruous."

"So far I fail to see anything even slightly unusual, let alone singular, about your experience," I remarked.

"I'm getting to the point," he said as he charged his pipe. "Once or twice during the trip, I looked up from the paper I was pretending to read and thought I caught the young man glancing at me. With my suspicions now aroused, I decided to disembark from the bus at Regent's Park and walk home from there. I was quite relieved when I descended to the pavement and watched the bus pull away with the young man still aboard.

"So, imagine my surprise when I turned onto Baker Street and saw the same fellow loitering in front of a shop across the way, pretending to study the contents of the store windows."

"Perhaps this was his destination all along," I suggested.

"I think not," replied my friend.

"Did you approach him?"

"No, I walked past him and continued to New Street where I turned and made my way to the alley which runs parallel to Baker Street. I entered through the rear – oh, by the way, Mrs. Hudson is making curried mutton for dinner – and then ran up here so that I might watch him unobserved from the front window."

While he was speaking, Holmes finished fiddling with his pipe and lighting it. Having said all this, he then took up a position perhaps two or three feet from the window so he could see without being seen.

"Is he still there?" I asked.

All of a sudden I heard Holmes laugh and then more to himself than me, he said, "Of all the unbridled cheek."

"Holmes, what happened?"

"The young man just looked up at the window, saluted me and then sauntered off down Baker Street as though he hadn't a care in the world. He might as well have shouted out and bid me 'Good day, Mr. Holmes.'"

"Do you have any idea what it means?"

"None whatsoever, but you may be certain that I intend to find out. The fact that he followed me here from my hidey-hole is most concerning."

I could certainly appreciate Holmes's disquiet. After all, not even I knew where his little burrows were located.

For the next several days, Holmes divided his efforts between keeping a watchful eye on Majors and, in his spare time, attempting to track down the young fellow. I knew with him it was a matter of pride. Although he had hardly been "defeated," a word he chose to apply to the encounter, I knew he felt he had been bested in some odd manner – and the list of people that could lay claim to having done that was a remarkably short one. In fact, he had once admitted to being beaten but four times – "three times by men and once by a woman."

I couldn't see where this was anything more than a mere trifle, but then I immediately recalled his telling me on more than one occasion, "There is nothing so important as trifles."

Finally, several days later, Holmes entered the flat perhaps a half hour before dinner. He said nothing, but I could tell he was vexed. A bit later, after lighting his pipe and settling into his chair, he looked at me and said, "I must admit to being at a complete loss, Watson. I have searched everywhere from here to Shadwell, but no one has seen the young man I am seeking."

"I think you are making entirely too much of this," I said. "You believe that you were followed on one occasion by a man you have not seen since, nor has your vast network of informants been able to discover his whereabouts – much less his identity. Perhaps he was simply an admirer. Is it not possible that you are mistaken?"

Holmes gave me a withering glance before he said, "No, Watson, I am not in error. Had you seen the insouciant manner in which he waved at me as he walked away, I am certain you would agree. It was as though he were saying, 'This round to me, Mr. Holmes.'"

The next morning as we were eating breakfast, Holmes was busy reading his letters from the first post of the day. He would finish one and then either drop it on the floor to be collected later and burned – a fate shared by the vast majority of his correspondence – or he would occasionally, read one a second time before disposing of it. Rarely, would he give a letter a third read, and on those occasions, he would place it on the table for future reference. On this morning, such was the case with the very last letter that he read.

I watched with fascination as Holmes perused the missive – once, twice, thrice. Finally, he handed it to me and asked, "Watson, what do you make of this?"

I took the letter and read it.

> *Dear Mr. Holmes,*
>
> *If you are free, I should like to call upon you this afternoon at half past three. If that time is inconvenient, I beg you to write me and suggest a more auspicious hour.*
>
> *I am contacting you on a matter of some urgency. I believe I can trust you as you did right by my sister several years ago.*
>
> *If I do not hear from you, I shall see you later today.*
>
> *Sincerely yours,*
>
> *Serena Erne*

Determined to apply the methods I had observed my friend employ on so many occasions, I began by stating, "Judging by the quality of the paper, I think it is safe to assume your correspondent must be fairly well-off."

Holmes said nothing but nodded.

"It was written by a woman, surely one who has been tutored – no doubt by an accomplished English governess – and as a result is obviously quite accomplished herself."

"Excellent," stated Holmes. "Continue, I pray you."

Having warmed to my task and bolstered by Holmes's praise, I carried on, "The script reflects a strong personality, and her choice of words and syntax would all seem to reinforce my deductions. She may even be a noblewoman." I paused, looked at my friend and asked, "How did I do?"

"Well, I agree that it was written by a woman and she may indeed be well-off, but I don't think the paper offers any insight into that. In fact, I shouldn't be surprised if the paper were provided by the hotel in which she is presently residing. Unfortunately, the absence of a watermark precludes my arriving at that conclusion with absolute certainty.

"As for her being schooled by a proper English governess, I am inclined to think she is American."

"American?"

"You mentioned syntax – when I see 'half past three' instead of the more common 'half three' followed by 'I beg you to write me' rather than 'to write *to* me' and shortly after we see the very colloquial 'I shall see you later today' rather than the more formal 'I shall call upon you' – I think we can safely dispense with the notion of a British governess and turn our sights towards the former Colonies."

I was too dumbfounded to reply. When I remained silent, Holmes asked, "Was there nothing else that struck you?"

Having embarrassed myself enough, I said, "Why don't you just tell me what else I missed?"

"It's not that you missed anything, but I must admit the name is rather suggestive."

"By the way, do you recall her sister?"

"No, in fact, I am quite certain I never handled a case for a woman with the last name of Erne."

"That may be the correspondent's married name," I suggested, "or perhaps her sister was wed and had a different surname when you assisted her."

"Those are certainly a possibilities," replied Holmes, "but I am inclined to view things from a slightly different perspective." He then turned and withdrew one of his yearbooks from the shelves without elaborating any further.

Feeling both chagrined and relieved that the letter was now behind us, I decided not to press my friend any further on the issue and just wait to see what the afternoon might bring.

The morning passed slowly, and after lunch I was so immersed in detailing "The Case of the Pernicious Publican" that I was quite startled to hear the bell ring. I glanced at my watch and saw that it was exactly half three. "If nothing else, this woman is certainly punctual," I thought. And it was just a moment later that our landlady knocked on the door and Holmes bade her enter.

"A young woman to see you, Mr. Holmes," said Mrs. Hudson. "She says her name is Serena Erne and she has an appointment."

"Indeed, she does, Mr. Hudson. Would be so kind as to show her up and perhaps put on the kettle?"

"Indeed, Mr. Holmes," she replied.

No sooner had our landlady departed than a moment later a woman tapped on the door. I went to answer, and Holmes followed me standing to my right. As she looked from myself to my flat mate, he said, "Do come in. I am Sherlock Holmes, and this is my colleague and friend, Dr. John Watson." After we had both shaken hands with her, Holmes extended his hand and taking her left hand in his right hand, he led her to what I had come to think of as the "client's chair." I had never seen Holmes act so courtly in the presence of a woman before. I thought that perhaps I had become a good influence on him.

Our visitor was dressed all in black, and I immediately assumed from her garb and the veil she was wearing that she was still grieving the loss of someone close. Although I could not see her face, she moved gracefully, suggesting she was younger rather than older. She was tall and slender. But beyond that I could deduce little else. Having seated her, Holmes then dropped into his usual chair opposite her.

After I had taken my seat, Holmes spoke to her saying, "In your letter you said that I was of some assistance to your sister; unfortunately, I cannot recall a client with the surname of Erne."

"That was not my sister's surname. Erne is my husband's name," she replied. "He passed away suddenly two months ago."

"Please accept my condolences on your loss," I murmured.

Although her diction was perfect and she had obviously studied elocution, there was no doubt from her utterances she was American.

"Well that certainly explains the confusion," I offered, smiling at her before I caught Holmes grinning at me.

Holmes then picked up the conversation. "If you would be so kind as to tell me your sister's name."

"It is not important," said our visitor. "She passed away several months ago."

"Again, my deepest sympathies," I said.

Not to be deterred, Holmes pressed on, "Still, for my own edification," he insisted. "You never know; perhaps she will have some bearing on the issue which has brought you hither."

"I fail to see how that could be possible," she replied.

At that moment, Mrs. Hudson knocked on the door. "Here is the tea you requested, Mr. Holmes. I've also brought up a basket with some blueberry scones which I baked this morning."

"Thank you, Mrs. Hudson," he said. Then turning to our visitor, he asked, "Perhaps you would care for some tea or a scone, Mrs. Erne?"

I suspected the tea was a ploy to get the woman to raise her veil. I'm certain Holmes was hoping that he might discern a family resemblance.

However, she declined the tea, and I could see a hint of frustration flit across my friend's face. However, he quickly recovered his composure and turning to our visitor, he asked, "Well then let us begin at the beginning and why don't you tell us what has brought you to Baker Street, Miss Serene Adler?"

Chapter Two

As you might imagine, I was more than a little taken aback by my friend's unexpected statement. After all our visitor had explicitly said her name was Serena Erne. She had also signed a note to that effect. For a split second I wondered if *the woman* had suddenly reappeared in our lives – and if so, to what end? However, before I could say anything to correct my friend or ask for clarification, the matter was taken out of my hands.

Our visitor suddenly lifted her veil, and for a moment, I could have sworn I was gazing once again upon the beautiful visage of Irene Adler. However, first impressions can be deceiving, and after a few seconds, I realized that despite the striking similarity, there were a few subtle differences. The face before me was a bit more careworn than Irene Adler's had been, and as I looked closer, I could see that she was older. Still, her resemblance to *the woman* was uncanny.

While those thoughts were racing through my mind, our visitor clapped her hands joyfully and exclaimed, "Marvelous, Mr. Holmes! Irene was certainly right in her assessment of your talents. Pray tell, what gave me away?"

"To begin with, your name."

"Her name?" I inquired.

"Come, Watson. Adler is eagle in German, and what is an erne but a sea eagle. Also Irene is derived from the Greek word for peace. It comes from Eirene, who was the goddess of peace. While Serena is derived from the Latin word *serēnus* from which we get tranquil or serene. Thus when I encounter, two such similarly named women both under rather enigmatic circumstances, well, I should think the conclusion is obvious."

"I should have known that wouldn't escape you, but it was another of my little tests. Your cunning might have impressed Irene, but I'm a skeptic. I had to see it for myself. Anything else?"

"When I led you to your seat, I held your hand, yet I could detect no wedding ring through your glove. Surely, a woman who has just lost her husband would still be wearing that token."

"Bravo," she said. "I have never been married, so you may call me Serena or Miss Adler, whichever you are more comfortable with."

Holmes ignored the last part of her sentence and asked, "Was following me in disguise recently another of your little tests?"

"My word, but you really are clever. Where did I slip up?"

Holmes ignored her question, and said, "My time is valuable, as I am certain yours is as well. So let us get to the point: Why have you been testing me, and, more to the point, why have you called upon me?"

Our visitor hesitated and then said, "If Dr. Watson's account is to be believed, you were ..." – and here she seemed to stop and search for just the right words – "an admirer of my sister."

"Indeed, she proved a more-than-worthy opponent and she plays the game with a certain panache which few others have been able to muster."

"It pains me to tell you this, Mr. Holmes, but I believe Irene is truly dead. That part of my story was not fiction. In fact, I suspect both she and her husband, Godfrey, have been murdered."

"Why have I heard nothing about it?" exclaimed Holmes. "Were their deaths reported in the papers?"

"Their deaths – if indeed they are dead – were not reported."

"Then what has led you to believe of their demise?"

Reaching into a small black reticule, she produced a letter. "Before you read this, there are certain things you should know about Irene.

"When the King of Bohemia referred to her as an 'adventuress,' he spoke better than he knew. Irene was always the wild one of the family. She was a year and a half older than I, and I looked up to her. I admired her. However, she frequently took chances – both with her career and offstage as well. Given her intelligence, charm, connections and entree into high society, she was often asked to do favours for certain highly placed individuals. Eventually her success attracted the attention of both the governments of the United States and the United Kingdom."

"So you're saying she was some sort of spy?" I asked.

"I suppose you could say that, but I believe the term she preferred was 'consulting arranger.'" As she uttered the phrase, she smiled at Holmes.

"What of the letter?" he asked.

She handed it to him and after he had read it through twice, he passed it along to me.

My Dearest Serena,

If you are reading this, you may assume the worst has befallen Godfrey and me. As I told you when I made these arrangements, if this letter comes into your possession, it is because I have not spoken to Neville in more than two weeks.

I don't want you to worry about me – whatever has happened, I brought it upon myself. However, if no word of me can be found in the papers, I should like you to contact Sherlock Holmes. Although we briefly crossed swords, I admired his ingenuity, courage and sense of fair play. If anyone will be able to ascertain what has happened to me, it will be he.

Before you contact him, please make certain that he has remained the same high-principled man who nearly outwitted me all those years ago. If I am any judge of character, I am certain you will find that he has changed little, if at all.

Please know that I love you and have always held you in the highest regard.

Your loving sister,

Irene

As you might expect, I was taken aback by the missive and my mind raced trying to figure out how Holmes would react.

"Where were your sister and her husband in the weeks before their ..." – here Holmes paused as though he were now searching for just the right word, finally he concluded with – "disappearance?"

"She and Godfrey had been touring the Continent. She had a number of engagements that took her to Milan where she performed at the Teatro alla Scala, The Real Teatro di San Carlo in Naples and the Palais Garnier in Paris. I think she hoped to return to London at some point, but she was always uncertain about how you might react. As a result, she kept putting the Royal Opera House off, despite the fact that Augustus Harris just kept offering her more money to appear."

"I am saddened to hear that," said Holmes. "She had nothing to fear from me. As I said, we matched wits briefly and she emerged victorious. I bore her no ill will."

I looked at my friend and I could see that the news – both of Irene Adler's death and her fear of returning to London – had touched him. However, Holmes being himself, that bit of melancholy quickly passed and when I glanced at him again a few seconds later, I saw a gleam in his eyes and that his features were set. It was a look with which I was all too familiar, and it boded ill for whoever might have brought harm to *the woman.*

"In her letter, she mentions a Neville. Have you any idea to whom she might be referring?"

"I was given to understand that from time to time she was employed by Her Majesty's government. Upon those occasions she would receive her orders and communicate her findings with those higher-up through a John Neville. He would always come to where she was, both here in England and abroad, because as I said, she felt a certain trepidation about returning to London."

"Did she give you anything to hold?" asked Holmes. "A package perhaps, or some other item."

"No, Mr. Holmes. The last thing I received from her was that letter with strict instructions that I was not to open it unless more than two weeks had passed without any type of communication from her. As you can see, she also wanted to make certain you were still the same man she had always admired.

"It has now been more than a month since I last heard from Irene, and that is why I am here."

"Well, it appears we have but one lead to follow," I offered, "We must locate this Neville fellow and see if he can shed any light on the fate of your sister and her husband."

"You have it exactly, old man," said Holmes. Then turning to Miss Adler, he said, "You have my word that we will learn what has become of your sister. If she should get in touch with you or something should occur to you, please feel free to contact me at any hour of the day or night."

"Where are you staying?" I asked.

"For the next week or two, I will be at the Langham Hotel. If I should move or decide to stay with friends, I will advise you before doing so."

No sooner had she departed then Holmes said, "I should have known!"

"What should you have known?" I asked, totally bewildered.

"That Mycroft was involved."

"Mycroft? That's a bit of a leap. What makes you say that?"

"You heard her say her sister would occasionally undertake assignments for the government. And we both know who functions as the government from time to time." After a moment he observed, "My brother always did have an eye for talent."

"But how would Mycroft have come to learn of her? Your brother is even less sociable than yourself and the thought of them making small talk about some cloak-and-dagger business over a chicken dish at a state affair is too ludicrous to even consider."

"Believe it or not Watson, my brother is an avid reader of *The Strand.*"

"You don't mean…" I replied as my words trailed off.

"I'm afraid I do, old man. I think it highly likely that Mycroft learned of Irene Adler through your short story, and I am certain that the idea of hiring a woman who had bested his brother was a temptation he found impossible to resist."

My short story "A Scandal in Bohemia," had been published in *The Strand* in June of 1891, shortly after Holmes had his confrontation with Professor Moriarty at the Reichenbach Falls. However, the editor had taken possession of it nearly a year prior and the events detailed in the story had occurred even earlier. "Oh, Holmes, I am so sorry," was all I could think to say.

"There is no need to apologize, old friend. She chose to work for Mycroft; she could just as easily have said no."

"But why accept such a position?"

"Mycroft can be very persuasive when it suits him to exert himself, and I am equally certain that money played no small role in the arrangement into which they entered. So as I say, there is no need for you to feel even the slightest remorse."

Although there was still a niggling sense of regret in the back of my mind, my friend's words had largely assuaged the guilt that had overwhelmed me initially. "What will you do next? Confront Mycroft?"

"No, I need to have proof; otherwise, Mycroft could simply say that I was sadly mistaken, and Neville was acting as a free agent. My brother will claim he knew nothing of his hiring of Irene. No, before we confront Mycroft, we must first speak with Neville, and I know just the man who can tell me where he is – or at least point me in the right direction."

"I assume you are referring to Langdale Pike."

"I am indeed, Come, he's probably at his usual spot in the bow window of his club on St. James Street."

I knew that Pike, who made his living as a gossip-monger for the more disreputable papers in London, had been of assistance to Holmes on many occasions in the past. Although I did not care for the man, I understood Holmes considered him as a reliable source of invaluable information.

After we had entered the club and the attendant had taken Holmes's card into Pike, we were quickly ushered into the front room where we joined the journalist at his table in the window. "Sherlock, it's good to see you, but it must be a matter of some note that brings you to see me in person instead of one of your little street urchins."

"It's good to see you too, Langdale. I must admit to having been terribly remiss in following up on my social obligations."

At that Pike began to laugh. After he had composed himself, he looked at me, grinned and said, "This has to be a matter of some urgency. In all the years I've known him, I have never heard Sherlock even attempt to make small talk."

I had to smile at the man's audacity and I could see Holmes fidgeting uncomfortably – again, something I never thought I'd witness. I began to wonder if there might be more to this friendship than I understood. Still, the ice had been broken, and Pike looked at Holmes and said, "What can I do for you, old friend?"

"I need to locate John Neville. It is a matter of some importance."

"Neville, the one who is employed by your brother?"

"The same," replied Holmes.

"Before we go any further, you do realize Neville is not his real name?"

"I rather suspected that," replied Holmes. "Although I am familiar with the man, having met him once or twice, I have never had to deal with him before on a personal level; as a result, that fact seemed rather insignificant. Since you are aware that Neville is a *nom de guerre*, is it safe to assume you know his real name?"

"Neville's true name is Frank Bortle. He has a room in Pall Mall somewhere, I believe, not too far from your brother."

I was rather taken aback by that revelation, but Holmes seemed the picture of equanimity. I wondered what types of assignments this Bortle fellow had carried out for Mycroft but decided to hold my tongue in the presence of Pike.

"Mr. Bortle doesn't happen to belong to your club, does he?" asked Holmes.

Pike snickered, "No, he's far too well-connected for this place. When he's in London, he often spends whatever free time he has up the street at White's."

"He must be well-connected," I thought. After all, White's was the oldest and one of the, if not the, most exclusive clubs in London. I was tempted to blurt out the quote from Disraeli's *Endymion* – The two things an Englishman cannot command – being made a Knight of the

Garter and a member of White's – but I decided to hold my tongue. Still, I thought that offered a bit of insight into Bortle and the circles within which he moved.

After a few more questions, we took our leave of the journalist, if indeed he can be called such, and when we were on the street, I turned to Holmes and asked, "What now?"

"As we are so close, I think a stroll along Pall Mall might prove invigorating – and quite possibly informative."

With that he turned on his heel and strode off in the direction of Pall Mall, where his brother lived, and where his brother's favourite haunt – The Diogenes Club – could be found. Along the way, we passed White's. From the outside it was a most prosaic looking building, but I had long ago learned not to judge anything by its appearance.

Although I was positively bursting with questions, I knew from long experience that Holmes would never discuss such sensitive affairs in public. As a result, I was well-aware my questions would have to wait until we returned to Baker Street – and even then, there was no guarantee I would receive any answers.

Chapter Three

Our stroll along Pall Mall proved fruitless as we sighted neither Mycroft nor Bortle, although I had no idea what the latter looked like. When we returned home, my friend despatched the boy in buttons with two telegrams and a letter. I busied myself looking back over my notes from the story I had titled "A Scandal in Bohemia." After I had finished refreshing my memory about our encounter, such as it was, with Irene Adler, I turned to the papers.

There appeared to be nothing that would interest my friend, but I was struck by a small item that mentioned how a farmer had returned from an extended trip abroad to his farm outside of Manchester only to discover that a large portion of the wheat crop had mysteriously shriveled and died. The man, whose family had been working the land for generations had no explanation for the unexpected mishap. The local constabulary was said to be investigating.

I thought to mention it to Holmes, but as he was engrossed in an experiment at his chemistry table, I continued reading the papers, and at some point I must have dozed off.

I was awakened by Holmes gently tugging on my sleeve. When I opened my eyes, he announced that Mrs. Hudson had prepared a dinner of steak and kidney pie, mashed potatoes and roasted greens. "I was thinking," he said as we sat down to eat, "that we might pay a visit to Mycroft at the Diogenes Club after we have finished dining."

Of course I agreed, and just as we finished our meal and I was just about to pepper Holmes with all the questions that had arisen during our visit with Langdale Pike that morning, there was a gentle rapping at the door. "Do come in, Mrs. Hudson," Holmes said.

At that, our landlady entered and before I could compliment her on the meal, she handed Holmes a note that had been sealed with red wax and stamped with a seal. As she handed him the missive, she said, "This just arrived by messenger. I was told it is quite important, and a reply is expected. There is also a cab downstairs should you accept."

"Thank you, Mrs. Hudson," replied Holmes. "Please tell the driver I shall let him know my plans forthwith."

"What is this all about?" I asked, as Holmes used his penknife to cut the wax seal.

"The letter is from Mycroft. I recognize both the wax and the seal." I watched as he read the letter over, but his expression remained stolid and gave nothing away. Finally, he said, "It appears my brother wishes to see us at the Diogenes Club on a matter of some urgency."

"What a coincidence," I exclaimed, "as we were planning to visit him anyway."

Holmes gave me a withering look and said, "You know I do not believe in coincidences. Something tells me Mycroft's summons is related to the visit paid us by Irene Adler's sister."

"Why on Earth would you think that?"

"Because I know my brother and what he is capable of far better than you, old friend. No, let us go see what he has to say for himself, but mark my words: The visit by Miss Adler and the summons from Mycroft are tied together in some way."

After donning our hats and coats, we descended the steps to find a fine growler, pulled by a pair of black stallions waiting for us. There was no crest on the cab door, but given what I knew about the Diogenes Club, I had hardly expected one.

Some thirty minutes later, we descended in front of one of London's most exclusive and certainly its most peculiar club. After Holmes had presented his card, we were shown to the Stranger's Room, the only location in the club where talking was permitted.

After several minutes, Mycroft entered the room and settled his portly frame into an over-sized wing chair. "So good of you to come, Sherlock," he said. "I suppose Dr. Watson is part and parcel of the arrangement."

"You suppose correctly, dear brother, and before you begin, I have a question for you. When did you first hire Irene Adler?"

Although I had not been in his company on too many occasions, I could see that Mycroft was taken aback by his brother's full frontal assault. After a moment or two, he answered, "I first became aware of Miss Adler back in 1887. The King of Bohemia asked me if the British government might be able to assist him in recovering a rather compromising photograph. I couldn't risk exposing Her Majesty's government to even a hint of scandal, so I suggested he contact you. After all, your work as a private citizen ..." and with that Mycroft trailed off.

"So, you learned she had bested me and decided to employ both her and her new husband?"

"Sherlock, please take this the right way. Anyone – man or woman – who could outwit you is someone I want working for me rather than against me. By recruiting her, I thwarted any possibility that I might encounter her as a foe in the future. I do apologize if my actions have touched a sore spot, but sometimes we are forced to do things we would rather not."

Holmes seemed mollified by his brother's words and the apology did seem sincere. Mycroft then broke the tension by offering us a taste of a delightful new single malt which had just made its way into the cellars of the Diogenes Club. After the drinks had been served, Holmes resumed his directness, "So why have you summoned me here? I know it wasn't to apologize."

Mycroft smiled ruefully, "I wish it were something that simple. I know you are familiar with the potato blight that destroyed the Irish economy nearly fifty years ago. I am also aware of your encounters with the Irish Republican Brotherhood[1] a few years back. Recently, it has been brought to my attention there is a monstrous plot to destroy the economy of the Empire by unleashing a similar blight capable of destroying England's wheat crop.

"I'm sure I don't have to go into detail about the damage which would result were such a plague unleashed."

"Odd," I remarked, "I read an article in *The Times* this morning about a farm outside Manchester where a portion of the wheat crop had shriveled and died under mysterious circumstances."

"I don't believe there is anything mysterious about it at all," stated Mycroft.

"A test of some sort?" inquired Holmes.

---

[1] The adventure to which Mycroft refers is related in *The Devil's Disciples: A Sherlock Holmes Adventure.*

"I believe so," replied Mycroft. "You may not be aware of this Sherlock, but several years ago a scientist by the name of Worthington G. Smith ..."

Holmes cut him off, "I am quite familiar with the work of Mr. Smith and I've long admired his botanical illustrations which appear regularly in the *Journal of Horticulture*. Exactly how is he involved here?"

"Smith is one of the leading experts on fungi. In 1884, he discovered *fusarium* head blight, a fungal disease that affects wheat and other small grains."

"Yes, I vaguely recall the article, but as it had no bearing on my work at the time, I gave it scant attention."

"Would that you had been more circumspect," replied Mycroft. "At any rate, we believe that a group of scientists, working on the Continent, in Germany, France and Italy, have taken Smith's work and made significant advances with it. As a result, they now pose a threat to the economy of the Empire, and given the nations we believe are involved, it behooves Her Majesty's government to once again ask for your assistance."

"What else do you know about this group? Who is funding them? Where are they based?"

"I'm afraid I really can't say anything further until you agree to undertake the assignment," replied Mycroft.

And so, we had arrived at a sticking point. As a rule, Holmes required his clients to tell him everything – and to be truthful about it – before he would agree to undertake an investigation. However, I could see Mycroft's hands were tied, and he seemed as inflexible as his brother upon that point.

A long, stony silence settled over the room, and I wondered how these two had settled their differences when they were younger. I knew Holmes to be a man of infinite patience when it suited him, and I wondered if his brother possessed that same trait and to the same degree. Holmes had already smoked one pipe and was in the midst of refilling another. Mycroft meanwhile was engrossed – or at least he pretended to be – in a copy of *The Times* he had picked up which had been lying on the table next to his chair. I had no idea when, or if, either one would give in, so finally I broke the silence by exclaiming, "We could be talking about how to save the Empire. The only problem is in order for that to happen, people actually have to begin speaking."

Holmes shot me a baleful look, but finally said, "Tell me what you can, Mycroft, and then I'll give you my decision."

"There's nothing more I can share without a commitment," Mycroft began, but when I scowled at him, he suddenly realized that a compromise of sorts could be reached. "As I said, we have come to believe a number of rogue scientists, at least two of whom had studied under Gregor Mendel, have been experimenting in Nord-Pas de Calais in France and the Po Valley in the province of Mantua in northern Italy, as growing conditions in both locations would be fairly similar to what they might encounter here. Although we cannot prove it, there appears to be a strong possibility they are being funded in one way or another by the German government."

"So, it would appear that there has been no rapprochement between the Kaiser and his uncle," observed Holmes.

"No, none at all. If truth be told, the relationship between His Majesty and her grandson has continued to deteriorate rather than improve."

Holmes thought for a moment then looked at me as if for confirmation. By way of reply, I gave a slight shrug, indicating the choice was entirely his.

Looking at his brother, Holmes said, "All right. What else can you tell us?"

Mycroft allowed himself the briefest of smiles and then said, "One of our agents first came across what he believed were the beginnings of a plot some two years ago. He works in the Cadastre in Paris, and became aware of several parcels of land being purchased in the Nord-Pas de Calais region."

"Cadastre?" I asked.

"It's the French equivalent of our own land registry office," murmured Holmes.

"Quite so," replied Mycroft. "At any rate, he was struck by the fact that these were mostly ancestral farms that were being sold, and in one or two cases leased, for what he considered exorbitant prices. His curiosity was further piqued when he learned that none of the plots abutted any of the others."

"So, no one was trying to cobble together pieces with the end result being a grand estate?"

"Exactly. As a result, we now believe that each plot was a testing area if you will. According to those living in the region, none of the farms has brought a wheat crop to market since they were purchased. Moreover, all seem to be closely guarded by both men with rifles and dogs. As you might expect, visitors are discouraged and trespassers do so at considerable risk to their person.

"After some discreet inquiries, we found an almost identical situation being played out in northern Italy."

"And in Germany?" my friend asked.

"To date, we have not been able to discern anything of a similar nature in either Germany or Prussia."

"How did Miss Adler and her husband become involved in this affair?"

If Mycroft were taken off-guard by his brother's question, he certainly didn't show it this time.

"We thought a beautiful woman might be able to gain access to at least one of the farms – a task none of our other agents had been able to bring to fruition. We had her and her husband rent a carriage with a wheel that had been tinkered with. When they broke down near the front gate of one farm and sought help, they were driven back into town. Their cart was repaired and returned to them the next day."

"These people do seem to value their privacy," I observed.

Mycroft continued as though I had not spoken. "We tried the same ruse a second time at another farm – the farthest away from the first – with exactly the same results."

"It sounds as though these men are well-trained, and they must be handsomely compensated. After all, Miss Adler can be quite persuasive when it suits her."

I wondered what might be running through Holmes's mind, for he was using the present tense and speaking as though Irene Adler were still alive and unmarried when we knew she had wed, and we had been led to believe that she had passed on.

"What did you do next?" asked my friend of his brother.

"We waited a week, and then Miss Adler suggested that she go out by herself. She felt that the men might feel less threatened by a woman alone as opposed to one traveling with a man."

"Surely you objected," said Holmes.

"I wasn't there, but according to the report filed by the agent …"

"That would be Neville, whose real name is Bortle?"

"How on Earth do you know that?" roared Mycroft.

"It's my business to know things," replied Holmes placidly. "So did Neville object?"

"Both he and Godfrey Norton were against the idea, but during lunch Miss Adler excused herself and never returned to the table. After some discussion, they checked with the ostler and found that she had left ten minutes earlier in a dogcart. Not knowing in which direction she was headed, they decided to wait for her to return. Unfortunately, after several hours, she still had not reappeared, so Norton went one way and Neville the other.

"When Neville returned to the inn a few hours later, Norton had yet to return. Uncertain what to do, he cabled me and I instructed him to keep watch. He remained in France for two weeks, scouring the back roads and making inquiries. However, he failed to turn up anything. For all intents and purposes, Miss Adler and her husband had vanished from the face of the Earth."

"You're certain they didn't just bolt for America or the Antipodes?" I asked.

"We've checked all the passenger manifests from Le Harve, Calais and Marseille. There are no records of couples matching their description embarking from any of those ports."

"They wouldn't travel as a couple," Holmes said, "especially if they suspected you'd be looking for them. Moreover, Miss Adler is quite a gifted actress and could have easily disguised herself as a man."

"Sherlock, she was quite talented, perhaps the most gifted agent I've ever employed, but more important – she was loyal, as was Godfrey. No, I'm afraid we must think the worst."

"Do you have any clue as to who might be in charge of this operation?"

"We have a list of suspects, and we are trying to eliminate as many as possible. As soon as I have something definite to share, I'll let you know."

"And what would you like me to do in the meantime? You summoned me here. Obviously, you have something in mind."

"I should like you and Dr. Watson to go to Manchester and look into the farm with the failed wheat crop. If something is amiss, I'm certain you will spot it."

"I may be able to help there," I ventured.

Both men turned to look at me and it was obvious from the expressions on their faces that they had quite forgot I was in the room.

"Do tell, Dr. Watson," said Mycroft.

"I have a cousin, Henry Francis Watson, who lives outside of Manchester. He owns a small farm with his wife and son, but as they were just getting by, he was forced to give up the soil and take a job at the docks on the new canal that opened a few years ago."

"That could certainly come in useful. Will he have any qualms about assisting in our endeavour?" asked Mycroft.

"Let's leave the innocents out of this," said Holmes in a rather stern voice. "This 'endeavour' of yours may have cost two lives already."

I could not tell if Mycroft were truly chastened or merely taken aback by his brother's commanding tone. However, he looked at Holmes and said, "You are quite correct, Sherlock. I have asked for your assistance, so I will let you decide how things are to be done."

"Excellent," replied Holmes, "I knew we could come to a meeting of the minds on this affair. Doctor Watson and I will prepare to visit his cousin – assuming, of course, he will have us."

"I'll wire him first thing in the morning." I said. "Although I really can't foresee any difficulty. I know both he and his son are quite taken with your adventures, old man."

"Before we leave, I should like to speak with Neville if that can be arranged," said Holmes. "He is in London?"

"Why don't you drop by here tomorrow afternoon at three o'clock. I'll have Mr. Neville waiting for you."

The brothers then began to discuss various other topics, and once again I was relegated to that of observer, contributing only occasionally.

In the carriage on the way home, I asked Holmes, "You don't think my cousin and his family will be in any danger, do you?"

"I shall do everything in my power to keep them as far removed from the fray as is humanly possible. Unfortunately, if the threat outlined by Mycroft has even a hint of truth to it, I feel we are all just a few steps away from anarchy and chaos. In short, the very fibre of life as we know it could soon be torn asunder. Hunger will drive men to the depths of desperation. We must make certain to eliminate this threat before it ever has a chance of becoming reality."

I have seen Holmes in many moods, from the jubilation of solving a particularly vexing case to the throes of despair on those few occasions when success had eluded him. However, there was a certain grimness in his voice as he spoke which I found most disquieting. It was a tone I had heard only once or twice before in our many years together, and I knew it did not bode well for those who would try to oppose him.

Chapter Four

The next morning I awoke to discover Holmes had risen early and left the flat. There was no note indicating where he had gone or when he might return. After I had eaten, I made my way to the telegraph office and dispatched a rather cryptic wire to my cousin.

> *Heading your way soon. STOP*
> *May we call upon you? STOP*
>
> *Cousin John*

I was certain that we would be warmly welcomed by my relative. After returning to Baker Street, I went up to my room and began to pack. When I had finished, I went back down to the sitting room, took my gun from my desk drawer and began to clean it. I had nearly finished when I heard Holmes's footfalls on the stairs. I left my work for later and went to sit at the breakfast table, hoping Holmes would apprise me of the success of his endeavours.

"You look as though you've had a busy morning," I said as Holmes hung up his coat and poured himself a cup of cold coffee.

"Indeed, one of my Irregulars followed Majors to a meeting, where he saw a long tube change hands. He then followed the other man back to his hotel. I contacted Inspector MacDonald, an arrest was made, and the Gough Map is now under lock and key at Scotland Yard, awaiting its return to the Bodleian Library."

"Well done," I exclaimed.

"Not entirely," he replied. "Majors will get away scot free. We have no evidence tying him to the theft and the man who bought the map is refusing to talk."

"It still sounds like a fine morning's work to me."

"Would that all our cases were solved so easily," he replied. "After leaving the Yard, I visited the Land Registry office in an attempt to learn about anyone who might have recently purchased a small farm outside of Manchester."

"And?" I inquired with a bit of trepidation in my voice.

"No parcels of land have been sold in the last two years."

"But how can that be?"

"I would suggest that the land had been leased rather than sold. I went back and found the article which stated simply that the farmer had returned from an extended trip abroad to discover the crop had failed. There is no mention of how long he had been away. I'm certain we will discover that he has been absent for several months if not a year or more."

Changing topics rapidly as he was wont to do, Holmes asked, "Have you received a reply from your cousin yet?"

"How do you even know that I have written to him?"

"Come, Watson, your best fountain pen is still in your jacket pocket. You use it only when you are writing up one of your lurid tales or when you are sending a telegram."

I had to smile. The pen had been the last gift my Mary had given me before she passed. Holmes was quite correct. I treasured it and used it sparingly.

"Not yet, I sent the telegram but an hour ago. If he is working, he may not read it until this evening when he returns from the docks."

"So then we must wait," said Holmes, who proceeded to drag down several of his commonplace books and pore over the articles in each intently. So engrossed was he in his research that he didn't partake of the sandwiches Mrs. Hudson brought up for lunch. Finally, after another hour had passed, he put the books down and said, "It's nearly time for my meeting with Mycroft and Bortle."

"Would you like me to accompany you?"

"No, old friend. I think it best if I go alone. You know how Mycroft can be when one of his agents is involved. I have no idea how long I may be. If you should hear from your cousin, my Bradshaw is here," he said, holding up the well-worn book and placing it on the table next to his chair.

"Depending upon when he replies, we may be leaving tonight or at the latest tomorrow morning. I will entrust all the arrangements to your most capable hands. And if you haven't finished packing," he said as he donned his coat, "you can do that as well."

It wasn't until after he had left, that I wondered how he knew I had begun to pack. I made a mental note to address that minor mystery when next I saw him.

It was perhaps half seven when a telegraph arrived from my cousin, Henry. He said he'd be glad to see us; unfortunately, he could not offer us the hospitality of his home as he had taken in a boarder. However, he did recommend a nearby inn, The Sawyer's Arms, that was not all that far from his house.

I consulted Holmes's Bradshaw and discovered there was a train leaving Euston the next morning at 9:23. There were only two stops – Rugby and Birmingham – and we would arrive in Manchester around half three in the afternoon. I considered sending the boy in buttons to reserve a carriage for us, but as I had yet to hear from Holmes, I refrained.

Finally, around 10 o'clock, I heard the front door open and Holmes ascend the stairs. He came into the room, and although I was quite curious as to how his meeting with Mycroft had gone, I refrained from badgering him and simply asked, "Whiskey or brandy?"

He smiled and said, "A brandy would be much appreciated." I poured two and placed his on the table next to him as he was busy charging his pipe – the old, oily briar. I sat and waited until he had lit the pipe with an ember from the fireplace and taken a sip of brandy. At that point, he looked at me, smiled and said, "You are indeed a patient man, Watson."

By way of reply, I merely nodded. "My meeting with Mycroft and Bortle was fairly unproductive. Bortle simply repeated what Mycroft had told us, adding a few more details when pressed."

"Was he able to provide any useful information?"

"Not a great deal. Prior to involving Miss Adler and her husband, Bortle had had two different men attempt to get work at the farms and both were sent away. However, one of the men, who was a native Frenchman and pretended not to speak any English, did overhear a driver of one of the wagons order his horse to '*hott*' or hurry."

"Another link to Germany?"

"So it would appear. Still, I'm not certain we can make too much of a single word, but it is thought-provoking to say the least." And then he changed topics and asked, "So what time are we leaving?"

"There's a train from Euston at 9:23 … Wait, a bit. How did you know we were leaving, and how did you know earlier that I had begun to pack?"

"When I returned this morning your pistol, a bore brush, solvent and a rag were on your desk. Obviously, you were in the process of cleaning and oiling your sidearm – something you always do last when we are preparing to leave. That's how I knew you had packed. At present, the top of your desk is positively pristine. Obviously, you have finished cleaning the gun and stowed it in your bag. Not a difficult chain to construct for one so well-acquainted with your habits."

We arose the next morning and after a quick breakfast, we set out for Euston. I was able to secure a first-class compartment. As you might expect, Holmes lapsed into silence whilst I watched the landscape gradually change from the dreary urban blight of London to the wide open green spaces of the countryside. Although Holmes had made me aware of his thoughts about the potential for horror in such a bucolic setting, I was nevertheless delighted by the sight of cows grazing in pastures and the quick glimpses of the rural hamlets as we sped by.

Mrs. Hudson had packed a selection of sandwiches, and after leaving Birmingham and departing on the last leg of our journey, I fetched a cheese sandwich which she had garnished with some spicy brown mustard. I was relishing my midday repast when Holmes observed, "If Mycroft is correct, such simple pleasures as sandwiches and scones may become luxuries in the near future."

The man has a special knack for killing my appetite. "Surely, it can't be as bad as all that."

"Wheat is the primary crop grown in England. Each acre farmed here yields approximately 25 bushels of wheat. If a blight were to destroy the English crop for even a year, it would be far worse than the potato famine that hit Ireland some 50 years ago. Imagine the economic strain on workers if such a staple had to be imported. Prices would rise significantly ... well I think you can see the threat to our nation is quite real if Mycroft is correct."

Having imparted this bit of good news, Holmes was once again his usual taciturn self. When we arrived in Manchester right on time, we hired a cab at the station and some ten minutes later we were in our rooms at The Sawyer's Arms. I despatched a messenger from the hotel to inform my cousin we had arrived. Perhaps an hour later, there was a knock on my door and the same messenger handed me an envelope and said, "He wrote a reply, sir."

I slipped the lad a few coins and opened the envelope to find a note from my cousin inviting Holmes and me to dinner that night at seven. I knocked on Holmes's door to inform him, but there was no answer. I couldn't imagine where he had got to, so I wrote him a note on hotel stationary and slipped it under his door. I considered going out to see a bit of the town but I was afraid I would miss Holmes, so I enjoyed a pint in the hotel taproom and then went to my room where I busied myself with a rather disappointing yellowback novel. The far-fetched plot failed to hold my interest, and I must have dozed off. Suddenly, I was awakened by a rather insistent rapping at my door.

I opened the door to find Holmes standing there. "Your note said dinner was at seven and it's now half six.

Since your cousin lives some twenty minutes away, I waited what seemed a reasonable bit before rousing you."

"Thank you, Holmes. I nodded off; just give me a few minutes to get ready." I splashed some water on my face, and then I turned to my friend. "You've been exploring – without me."

"We need to keep a low profile for the foreseeable future, so I went out in disguise to get the lay of the land. It's a most interesting city although these Mancunians speak a language that at times seems only distantly related to English."

I was still somewhat miffed at having been left behind, but I quickly got over it. I was anxious to see my cousin and his family. As we left the hotel, I purchased a bouquet of flowers for his wife and then we boarded a cab. We headed east and crossed the River Irwell and made our way towards Eccles. We arrived at my cousin's house just about 30 minutes later. As we alighted from the cab, Holmes spoke to the driver, "If you can be back here around ten, I'll double your usual fare to take us back to the hotel."

"Right," he replied. "There's a pub, The Angry Drake, about a half mile down the road, I'll be there should you decide to return early."

After knocking on the door, we were greeted warmly by Henry; his wife, Clara; and their 12-year-old son, David, and then we were introduced to his tenant, Nicholas Tagliamonti, who we were told also worked at the docks. Clara was thrilled with the flowers, and although he was uncomfortable, Holmes was the center of attention as both Henry and David peppered him with questions and occasionally Tagliamonti would chime in as well.

After dinner, Henry, Holmes and I retired to my cousin's study. After we had caught up on old times, I asked my cousin about his boarder. "He's only been with us about six weeks, but he was a godsend. I was at the end of my rope with the farm when he came looking for a room, and we needed the extra money. He also helped me get a job at the docks when I realized I couldn't make a go of it." Henry then informed us that Tagliamonti had come to England as a boy. His father had run afoul of a local gang in Italy, so the man had fled with his wife and Nicholas, who was an infant at the time, to England.

I noticed that Holmes was paying close attention to the conversation, but I had never known him to be reticent during an investigation. Eventually, Henry asked what had brought us east, and before I could answer, Holmes replied, "I'm mixing business and pleasure. I'm looking into possible connections between the scuttlers here and a gang in London, but I'm also hoping to take advantage of some of the great fishing spots in the area. I've heard wonderful things about Curley's Trout Fishery."

"And they are all true, but you may want to stay at an inn near there, it's a good twenty miles away, and save yourself the time getting there from Manchester. After all, the early bird catches the worm and the early worm catches the fish.

"As far as the scuttlers are concerned, a word of caution, Mr. Holmes. They are serious lads and plenty vicious to boot. They'll have nowt to do with the police. In fact, rumour has it that there's more than one copper in their pocket."

"So then it's better that we are staying in town, I wouldn't want any of this to find its way to your doorstep," Holmes said.

Although my cousin denied he was concerned, I could see that Holmes's words had struck a nerve. When we left after a nightcap, the cab was waiting for us in front of the house.

No sooner had we settled ourselves, then I asked Holmes, "How did you know about the scuttlers and Curley's Trout Fishery?"

Holmes just gave me a look and answered my question with one of his own. "Did you notice anything unusual about Mr. Tagliamonti?"

"Now that you mention it, he didn't have any noticeable accent."

"If he were brought here as an infant, I wouldn't expect him to have one. Did nothing else strike you?"

"No, he seemed a perfectly pleasant chap. What are you driving at, Holmes?"

"Did you notice a portion of a tattoo of a flame on the back of his right hand?"

"I can't say that I did. Is it significant?"

"It may prove to be. Do give it some thought, old man. Perhaps something will strike you."

I pondered my friend's question as we drove back to The Sawyer's Arms. When we had ascended to our rooms, I said to Holmes, "I have a bottle of brandy with me if you'd care for a final nightcap."

He accepted and as we sat in a convivial silence, I wondered where this case would take us next.

Suddenly Holmes turned to me and said, "This simply won't do. Your cousin is correct. We are too far from the farm, and I need to see what has transpired there. Tomorrow, after breakfast, we will set out for Curley's Trout Fishery, which is about a mile from the farm and take rooms at an inn near there as Henry suggested."

He looked at me for a second and then said, "I could go alone and that would allow you more time for a visit. This is going to be a simple reconnaissance mission, so if you'd prefer to spend the evening with Henry, I'll certainly understand."

"And if anything should happen to you, I'd never forgive myself. Moreover, if I should decide to chronicle this adventure someday, I'd like my readers to understand that I was involved from the beginning until the end."

"Good old Watson. I know you have my best interests at heart but …"

I cut him off before he could continue. "The matter is no longer up for discussion, Holmes. Besides, I like angling as well as the next fellow – and I especially enjoy fishing for trout."

And so it was that after a hearty breakfast, the next morning, I found myself asking the hotel manager if he could recommend a decent inn near Curley's. Holmes had asked me to make the arrangements while he tended to a few errands. The manager told me that a good friend owned an inn called The Ewe and Cry and that I should mention his name. He also arranged for a driver to take us to the inn and to pick us up three days later at noon.

About thirty minutes later Holmes returned carrying two cases that I knew contained fly rods as well as two creels. I had to smile in spite of myself. "We can't very well show up to go trout fishing without rods, can we? Also, the creels are filled with a selection of lures guaranteed to attract the biggest fish in the water."

During the ride to the inn, I asked Holmes, "Why the masquerade? And why trout fishing?"

He smiled and said, "As I said, the farm in which I am interested is but a mile from the reservoir where we'll be fishing. I'm counting on you to cover for me, should it become necessary, while I do a bit of exploring."

I wondered how many other steps Holmes had taken to secure any advantage he might get in this investigation. We rode in silence for quite some time before my friend glanced at his watch and said, "We should be at the inn in about 30 minutes. After we have taken our rooms, let's explore the town and see what we can learn. The real work will begin tomorrow morning."

We arrived at The Ewe and Cry just about a half hour later. We checked in using the names Hudson and Wiggins. After we had signed the register, the clerk said, "I believe I have a telegraph for you Mr. Hudson," and with that he handed Holmes the wire. After we had stowed our gear, I knocked on Holmes's door. He bade me enter, and no sooner had I shut the door then I asked, "Who could have sent you that telegram? No one knows we're here."

"Mycroft knows. I gave him our full itinerary before we left London."

"But I only found out about this inn, this morning."

"Indeed, but I knew about it several days ago. In fact, Mycroft had two men staying here who checked out rather unexpectedly this morning."

"But why?"

"I had to be certain that we'd be able to get rooms."

"Holmes, I'm beginning to think you don't trust me."

"Not at all, old friend. It's just that mendacity is not in your make-up. Sadly, and I'm not proud of it, but it's as natural to me as combing my hair or filling my pipe."

"Obviously," I said, not in the least mollified by his half-hearted admission of a personal weakness.

"Well, what did Mycroft say?"

Holmes handed me the telegram, which I unfolded and read. It was short but terribly frightening.

SECOND FARM, SAME SITUATION, COTSWOLDS. M

"What does it mean?" I asked.

"It means time is of the essence, my friend."

Chapter Five

We ate breakfast the next morning at the hotel, and then immediately set out for Curley's. After swearing us to secrecy, the manager had given us directions to what he maintained was the best fishing spot on the lake. He also told us that the "lake" was actually an old reservoir. After a hike of perhaps two miles, we arrived at our destination.

When we had selected a secluded spot quite close to the manager's preferred site, Holmes informed me that the farm in question was about a mile distant from the far side of the lake. "I need you to hold down the fort, old man. Can you manage two rods? If anyone should wonder why you are fishing for two, you can tell them I am indisposed at the moment." As the only other people we had seen were in a small boat at the other end of the lake, I felt pretty confident I could handle any situation that might arise.

With that he strode purposefully off towards the far side of the lake. In ten minutes he was out of sight. After a bit of practice, I found myself able to handle both rods with a fair degree of aplomb. Before an hour had passed, I had caught two good-size trout and was thinking about dinner that evening. Another forty-five minutes passed, and I was just beginning to worry about Holmes when I saw him approaching in the distance.

"Well?" I asked when he had rejoined me.

"It's an incredible sight to see, Watson. Whole fields of wheat discoloured and shriveled. There'll be no harvest this year for certain and perhaps next year as well. I collected some of the kernels and spikelets to study," he said pulling two envelopes from his inside jacket pocket. "I can only assume the blight contains some type of toxin that arrests growth and results in the discolouration of the straws. I also discovered what I believe are spore masses on many of the infected plants. This bodes ill for the Empire unless we can capture those involved and find a means of destroying the blight."

"What then do you make of that second farm in the Cotswolds?"

"Given that it is located more than one hundred miles from here, it would suggest they are still experimenting and didn't want to take the chance of one test crop infecting another." He paused and then added, "In a way, that may be good news."

"Really?" I replied, stunned by my friend's pronouncement.

"Yes, it would suggest they are still growing and testing various strains of blight, and if that is the case, we still have a chance to quash this plan before it goes much further."

"I can only hope you are right. What is our next move?"

"We need to return to London as quickly as possible and see what else, if anything, Mycroft has discovered."

"I suppose dinner here is out of the question?" I asked, proudly holding up my catch which had grown to four beautiful fish.

"I'm afraid so, old man, but I'm certain the innkeeper will appreciate your largesse."

With that we hiked back to the inn where Holmes made arrangements for a wagon to take us to the rail station in Manchester. We arrived at the station a few hours later and learned that we had an hour wait until the next train. I wrote a letter to my cousin thanking him for his hospitality and explaining we had been summoned back to London unexpectedly. I posted it from the station shortly before the train arrived.

As you might expect, much of the trip back to London was spent in silence. Holmes was in a pensive mood and puffing furiously on his pipe. I was also buried in my own thoughts wondering how this all might play out. At one point, I had to leave the cabin as the air had become positively unhealthy. When I returned sometime later, I found Holmes much as I had left him. I wondered if he had even noticed my absence, but I was relieved to discover that he had opened the window a bit.

I looked at my watch after we had left Rugby and realized that we would arrive home in about ninety minutes. From the other side of the car, I heard Holmes say, "I'm sorry about the smoke, old friend. But you know this has proven to be even more vexing than a normal three-pipe problem."

"Not to worry, I just needed some fresh air. I was afraid I was going to die in here from asphyxiation. Given how much milder my tobacco is, it wasn't as if I could fight fire with fire."

"No, I suppose not," he declared as he chuckled and then he grew serious again. At one point, I looked up from the novel I was reading and saw Holmes staring at me, and then just as quickly his eyelids drooped and I wasn't at all certain that I hadn't imagined the entire incident. As we were pulling into the station, Holmes suddenly came to life. He looked at me and asked, "Can you take the bags to Baker Street? I must find Mycroft," – and here he glanced at his watch – "although I am fairly certain I know exactly where he'll be." With that he dashed off. I've said it before, the man can be absolutely maddening at times.

Mrs. Hudson was surprised at our return, saying, "I thought you'd be away for another two or three days."

"Holmes had to hurry back to London," I explained, and as she left, I thought I could hear her muttering to herself.

It was around nine o'clock when Holmes finally reappeared. "You've missed supper," I stated, "shall I ask Mrs. Hudson to prepare some sandwiches?"

"No, but a pot of strong coffee would be much appreciated. I have a great deal of reading to do tonight."

I went down and asked Mrs. Hudson for the coffee and a sandwich as well. When I returned upstairs, Holmes had thrown himself into his chair and covered the floor around his seat with books. "What did Mycroft have to say?"

"He informed me he had confirmed that similar incidents have occurred in a number of isolated farms in both Italy and France."

"My word! Does the Kaiser think he can bankrupt all of Europe?"

"I have no idea what the Kaiser thinks; in fact, I'm wondering if he is even aware of the extent of these experiments and the danger they pose not only to England's economy but to the world's as well."

"Did you give Mycroft the samples you took from the field?"

"I gave him half of each, and he promised to put his top scientists on the case while I kept some to examine myself," he said as he pulled the envelopes from his inside pocket.

We sat there in silence for a few moments until Mrs. Hudson knocked on the door. "Come in, Mrs. Hudson," said

Holmes. As she entered, he rose and took the tray from her. "Thank you, dear lady. You are a true angel of mercy."

She smiled and said, "I'm glad you're back, Mr. Holmes. Oh, this arrived for you yesterday. It was delivered by that young woman who stopped here several days ago. She instructed me to place it into your hands and not to leave it anywhere where it might be misplaced."

She handed Holmes a cream-coloured envelope and then excused herself. "It didn't take Serena Adler long to take the cut of your jib," I said.

"Come, Watson, you know that I can lay my hands on anything I desire within minutes – provided, of course, that you and Mrs. Hudson haven't indulged in your passion for fastidiousness."

I had to admit there was a certain truth to Holmes's words, but I certainly wasn't going to admit it. "What does the letter say?"

He pulled a sheet of notepaper from the envelope and read:

Dear Mr. Holmes,

I just received an envelope from Irene. It was addressed to me in America and has only just arrived. When I opened it, I found a letter addressed to Dr. Watson. I don't know what to make of it, so I sent it along to you. I trust that you will see that Dr. Watson receives it.

Sincerely,

Serena Adler

With that, he withdrew a second somewhat smaller envelope. I could see that it was addressed to myself. To say I was nonplussed would be an understatement. I had never met Miss Adler in person, so I had no idea why she would be communicating with me.

Holmes passed the envelope to me, and then stood there expectantly. Having the upper hand, if only for a moment, I said, "This might be a matter of some delicacy, Holmes."

"Given the fact that you and Miss Adler have never actually met, I find it highly unlikely that it contains a billet-doux. Come now, old friend, I'm more inclined to think that letter is intended for me but she sent to you in case her mail were being intercepted."

"But the English postal service is secure, is it not? And I am just as certain that the Americans are equally circumspect, if not more so, with letters that are posted."

At that Holmes laughed. "Secure? I should say not. I willingly admit to having slipped postmen a few quid upon occasion to see where letters had been sent."

"Holmes!" I said in feigned indignation.

"Come, old man. Open the letter and let us see what the late Miss Adler has to say to you."

I went to tear open the envelope, but before I could Holmes handed me his penknife and said, "Please, use this." I took the blade and slit the top of the envelope which I then handed to Holmes. As I read over the letter he took out his lens and carefully examined the envelope. When I had finished, I turned to Holmes and said, "I have no idea what to make of it. Perhaps something will strike you."

As I handed him the letter, he thrust the envelope and his lens into my hand and said, "Please examine this carefully and let me know what you see."

I have reproduced the letter below:

Dear Dr. Watson,

I have been meaning to write to you for some time. I must say I was quite flattered by your depiction of me in your short story, "A Scandal in Bohemia." I must also thank you for referring to me as "the late Irene Adler." You are truly a dear. I cannot tell you how many times it has saved me from awkward explanations about my name and identity. However, I might take issue with your description of me as being "of dubious and questionable memory." I would hope that you understand that last remark was intended in jest.

Now to business: I have read everything that you have written and was particularly taken with your tale about Sir Henry Baskerville. I could swear that I have read it at least five times, and I am certain I will read it at least five more. In fact, I have fond memories of devouring it in one afternoon while I was on holiday at a small croft in Scotland. I have no doubt I'll read it again in the not-too-distant future. Somehow, it struck a cord with me.

I believe I also devoured "The Copper Beeches" that same day. Such a lovely name for an estate.

*Please extend my
regards to Mr. Holmes. Once again I want
express my appreciation for treating me so
fairly in your depiction, and you may rest
assured I shall continue to look forward to
all of your literary endeavors. I do hope
you continue to find success and that
inspiration continues to strike you when
you are most in need of it's uplifting forces.*

Sincerely yours.

Irene Adler

*PS As Mr. Holmes might say, "There's
nothing new under the sun."*

Holmes read the letter at least twice while I turned his lens upon the envelope. When he had finished, he looked up at me and said, "What do you make of the envelope?"

"I'm not sure what you mean. The paper and envelope both seem quite dear and as you can see, it was sealed when it arrived, so it obviously hasn't been tampered with."

"I see nothing of the sort; in fact, I see exactly the opposite," my friend replied with a slight degree of exasperation. "Look at this flap carefully, you can just make out very faint traces of glue beyond the flap which tells me this envelope has been steamed open and resealed. Had it not been opened, no glue would be visible. Moreover, I can detect just the slightest musty odor, which again indicates that it has been steamed open and resealed."

Putting the lens to the paper once again, I could discern a very thin line of glue in two different spaces. Chagrined, I had to admit that, as Holmes had so often reminded me, I had seen but I had not observed.

When I looked up at him, he smiled knowingly, and asked, "The letter itself? What do you make of that?"

"It seems terribly innocuous – except for the unfortunate grammatical lapses in the middle and at the end. I should have expected better of Miss Adler but then homophones are the bane of many writers. I can't believe she confused cord and chord."

"By Jove, Watson! I think you've hit it. Consider the text of the letter carefully. Miss Adler does not misspell any words, nor does she make any grammatical errors except for the three to which you allude. As a musician, I am certain she would never use cord for chord. Moreover, she uses the pronoun 'I' some 13 times – and in every instance but one, it is followed by an auxiliary verb. At the end of the second paragraph, she opts for the contraction 'I'll.' She follows that in her post script by employing 'their's – another contraction. "

"What has all that to do with her misuse of homophones?"

"I think her grammatical lapses were deliberate. She used the incorrect 'cord,' 'its' and 'their's' in a subtle effort to draw our attention to the single contraction 'I'll' which is also a homophone for aisle or isle."

"How does that help us? London is filled with aisles in churches, stores, theaters and the like and both the Thames and the Channel have their fair share of isles; in fact, there are more than a hundred islands in the Thames alone."

Holmes gazed at me and merely said, "Consider the rest of the letter."

"There's not much in the way of specifics," I said. "She refers to 'A Scandal in Bohemia,' *The Hound of the Baskervilles*, a croft in Scotland, and 'The Copper Beeches.'"

"So close," murmured my friend.

And then it hit me, "The Isle of Dogs. She mentions 'Scandal' and 'Copper Beeches' by name but simply alludes to *The Hound* by mentioning one of the characters."

"Bravo!" he exclaimed. "She doesn't refer to the hound but only to Sir Henry."

"Nor does she refer to anyone in 'Copper Beeches,' but both do involve rather dastardly canines.

"Yes, no doubt she was hoping we would catch the allusions and whoever was reading her mail wouldn't. But how on Earth was she able to post it? And how did she come to learn of it or suspect it?"

"I'm afraid those are questions only Miss Adler can answer – if she is still alive. More important, however, is the fact that at last we have a definite lead."

"Indeed, and one that is relatively close to hand," I added.

"It makes perfect sense," Holmes continued. "They'd need a laboratory to conduct their experiments – and one located in a place where they could be assured a certain degree of privacy and ready access to whatever supplies they might require. Also, they could travel upriver into the heart of England when their plan comes to fruition. It's a brilliant and daring move."

"Also, given the varied backgrounds of London dockworkers, a German accent would be no more out of place than that of an Irishman or an Italian," I added.

"Exactly," Holmes said. "It would appear our adversaries are employing the age-old stratagem of hiding in plain sight."

"So what do we do next? Contact Mycroft? Inform Lestrade?"

"I think for the moment it is best if we keep our own counsel. Just as there are multiple farms at which they are testing the blight, there may be more than one laboratory in more than one location. If this one should be discovered, they might simply close it down and move to the next one. There is also the possibility that someone in Mycroft's employ has been compromised."

"You don't really think that?"

"I think for the moment it would be best if we remember the sage advice of Mr. Kipling:

Down to Gehenna or up to the Throne,
He travels the fastest who travels alone."

"I know you pride yourself on seldom being wrong, but I must say I truly hope you are this time and there is only one lab and none of Mycroft's agents has been compromised."

"Seldom?" inquired Holmes archly, and then he chuckled. "It's a good thing your readers aren't aware of my many missteps."

I was taken aback. Holmes expressing a degree of modesty. And then it hit me that this was a situation that could not be taken lightly, and he was putting on a brave face. Of course, he could have been totally serious. Sometimes with Holmes one never knows.

"And now, Watson, you to bed. I have a great deal of reading to do, and we have a busy day in front of us tomorrow."

I turned to go to my room and looked back to find Holmes already immersed in a periodical he had fetched from the floor.

I thought about bidding him good night but decided against it as I had no wish to disturb his concentration. As I readied for bed, my mind was swirling with thoughts of the grave threat posed by the tiny spores. As a medical man I was acutely aware of the havoc an infection, caused by invisible germs and bacteria, could wreak on the human body, and as I tossed and turned thinking about barren fields and shriveled stalks of wheat, my mind turned to the thousands of "coffin ships" desperately fleeing Ireland during the famine – unseaworthy, unsanitary, overcrowded and riddled with disease. Although I am not a religious man, I prayed to the Almighty that England would be spared a similar fate.

Chapter Six

The next morning I dressed and came downstairs to find Holmes sitting at the table disguised as a navvy. He looked like a disreputable tar, and once again I was impressed with the ease with which my friend could become the character he was playing.

"I assume you are heading to the docks this morning?"

"You assume incorrectly, matey! *We* are heading to the docks."

"Holmes, while dress-up suits you, I'm really not cut out for that sort of thing."

"Then you'll be pleased to know you can go dressed as you are."

"I don't understand."

"I want you to wait an hour after I leave. Enjoy your breakfast. Then I want you to take a cab to the docks at the Isle of Dogs and go from warehouse to warehouse pretending to look for a shipment of coffee that has gone missing." Pushing a piece of paper across the table, he added, "I've prepared a bill of lading for you that should pass muster."

"And what exactly am I really looking for?"

"Anything out of the ordinary – a warehouse with too few workers, one with too many guards – in short, anything that strikes you as being unusual or out of place. I have infinite faith in you, Watson."

"I won't let you down, but while I'm doing that what will you be doing?"

"The exact same thing – only from a very different point of view." He laughed dryly, finished his coffee and said, "We'll meet back here tonight at six to compare notes."

He then picked up a baling hook that had been resting on the floor and headed towards the door humming a melody of some sort – presumably a sea chantey – although I didn't recognize the tune.

I lingered over breakfast and when Mrs. Hudson came to clear the tray, I informed her that neither of us would be home for lunch but that she could expect two hungry men for dinner.

"One hungry man, at least," she replied. "Mr. Holmes eats like a bird – if at all – when he is working on one of his cases." As proof, she pointed to Holmes's untouched breakfast plate. "See what I mean?"

I apologized for Holmes, thanked her for her forbearance and made my way to the street where I hailed a cab. "The Isle of Dogs," I told the cabbie, and as we headed towards the Thames, I reflected upon my destination.

The Isle of Dogs is something of a misnomer, as that particular piece of land is not actually an island but rather a peninsula jutting out into the Thames. I had been there on a number of occasions to watch the Millwall Athletic Football Club play several matches. I had also flown by it one night in a police launch as we pursued Jonathan Small and the Aurora down the Thames.

In recent years, the shipping industry, always prevalent in that area, had broadened its presence with the construction of a number of new wharves by the West India Dock Company. Now, it was quite busy. I wondered as I proceeded along the East India Dock Road whether the electric lights that had been installed at the Royal Albert Dock some years back had made the short journey east to the Isle of Dogs. I supposed I'd find out soon enough.

I finally alighted at Westferry Circus and made my way to the South Dock. Attired as I was, with cravat and waistcoat, I looked and felt out of place among the more poorly dressed stevedores and other labourers, but they paid me no mind. I entered the first warehouse and could see nothing amiss. Business was being carried on and the buzz of commerce was almost palpable. I was pleasantly surprised to see the warehouse aglow with electric lights and I wondered how long it would be before every home in London could enjoy such a luxury.

As you might expect, no one knew anything about my missing shipment of coffee, and so I repeated my inquires at the next warehouse and the one after that and the one after that. By mid-afternoon, I had visited some eighteen warehouses and seen nothing amiss. I noted that some six of the warehouses had electric lights while the remainder were lacking the latest convenience.

There were two such buildings I was unable to enter as they were both securely locked. However, I didn't see any guards so I just assumed that those two import companies had gone out of business. There was also one other noteworthy structure, along with a number of smaller outbuildings, that had nothing to do with shipping.

A large sign proudly proclaimed in gleaming gilt letters:

The Electrical Power Storage Co., Ltd.,
Storage Battery Makers by Warrant
To His Majesty The King

I guessed the various warehouses would soon all have electric lights – powered either by cables or batteries. With that thought in mind, I returned to the two buildings that had been locked. I was looking to see if I could discover any discarded power cells, but there was nothing to indicate that batteries were being used at either location, nor had electrical wires been run to the buildings.

I spent another twenty minutes looking for anything that appeared out of place, but everything seemed quite ordinary. Disappointed in myself, I returned to Baker Street where I enjoyed an afternoon sherry and then dozed off while I was waiting for Holmes. Sometime later, I felt a hand gently shake me, and I heard a voice say, "Watson, it's time for supper."

I awoke to find Holmes standing over me. He had doffed his disguise, washed and donned his blue dressing gown. "You won't believe what Mrs. Hudson has prepared for dinner."

"Oh?"

"She has outdone herself," he exclaimed. I wandered over to the table where I discovered that she had grilled two whole trout which she had stuffed with lemons and herbs until they were charred and smoky and flaky. She served them with asparagus, boiled potatoes and corn.

"How could she have known?" I asked.

I then looked up to see Holmes smiling at me and said, "Thank you, Holmes."

"It was the least I could do," he replied. "Tell me how did your day at the docks go? I hope it went better than mine."

"Oh?"

"Yes, I was hired to unload a freighter just in from Japan. The crew was a mix of nationalities and the foreman was a hard taskmaster, so I was unable to sneak away. As a result, I learned nothing."

"So, you were forced to do an honest day's work," I laughed.

Holmes replied with a sardonic smile.

Sensing it was my time, I said, "Well, to begin with, no one knew where my missing coffee could be found, but I may have discovered something promising."

"Do tell."

I described for him in detail the two locked buildings and the nearby Power Storage Company building. I then began to tell him how most of the warehouses were now powered by electricity, and then I voiced my suspicion that perhaps one or both of the buildings, although they appeared to be without power, might be employing batteries.

"Would a laboratory such as the one we seek need electricity? And if it does, could batteries generate enough electricity?"

"Bravo, Watson! I cannot answer your questions with certainty, but I should think that is a line worth investigating." At that Holmes jumped up from the table and strode to his desk. "Let me send a note to Mycroft at the Diogenes Club and see how soon he replies." Holmes then dashed off a quick missive, summoned the boy in buttons – instructing him to inquire if a reply were possible – and then despatched the lad with all due haste, giving him money for a cab to and fro.

"We'll soon discover if omniscience is indeed Mycroft's forte."

With that we both attacked our dinners with gusto. The silence that followed was an amiable one – broken intermittently by bits of banal chatter. It seemed almost as if everything hinged on Mycroft's reply – and in a certain sense it did.

It was perhaps an hour and a half later that I heard a gentle rapping on the door. "Come," ordered Holmes and the lad he had despatched entered bearing an envelope. "I had to wait for a while, but then the man said to get this to you as soon as possible and he even gave me more money for a cab," he said excitedly. Holmes instructed the boy to keep the extra and then said, "You've done well, my lad."

Once the boy had closed the door, Holmes tore open the envelope. I watched as he read the note and then he looked at me and said, "According to the scientist with whom Mycroft is working, this particular strain of blight, *Fusarium graminearum,* does not require a great deal of light in order to thrive – only two or three days."

"Well, there goes that theory," I sighed.

"Hold a bit," Holmes said, "Mycroft also says that germination does best in warm, humid conditions. Perhaps they've created a greenhouse of sorts powered by lights and one of those new electric heaters that the American, Mr. Edison, has invented."

"Do you think such a thing is possible? Here in London? It would cost a small fortune."

"If a small fortune led you to a much larger prize, might it not be worth the risk?"

"I suppose so."

"Care to join me on another trip to the docks? I am curious to see if there is any light emanating from a certain warehouse that has apparently been under lock and key all day."

I readily agreed and after we had changed into dark clothing. Holmes took up his stick and a dark lantern. He then looked at me and said, "You might want to bring your revolver, old friend. As you are all too aware even the most innocent expeditions can go sideways without warning."

I patted the pocket of my jacket, smiled and said, "I am all too aware of how any number of my forays with you have ended up."

We took a cab back to Westferry Circle. Although the docks were less busy than they had been earlier in the day, there was still a fair number of laborours milling about, putting in a full day's work under the never-dimming glare of Thomas Edison's gift to mankind.

When we finally reached the warehouses, both of which were located quite close to each other at the far end of the pier, things had got considerably darker, and I was glad we had brought both a dark lantern and my pistol. There appeared to be no one about, so after carefully reconnoitering the area, Holmes and I approached the first of the structures I had noted. There were only two windows on each side of the building, and Holmes and I started at the rear.

"The warehouse appears to be dark," I observed.

"Appears is precisely the word, Doctor. If you look carefully, you can see that these windows have been papered over from the inside. Obviously, they are desperate to conceal their doings from the casual passerby. In fact, if you examine this window closely," he said, shining his light directly on the pane, "you can see that this glass has been reinforced with wire. What could be so valuable in an empty warehouse that would require such extra protection?"

"I have no idea," I replied.

"I do, but I can only hope that I am proved wrong this time," he said grimly.

We then moved to the next window and encountered the same thing. Within a few minutes we had checked all the windows and discovered that they had all been masked with some sort of material from the inside.

"What's our next move?" I asked.

"Let's take a look at the lock on the front," Holmes said softly. We then returned to the front but when Holmes shone his dark lantern on the lock, he murmured, "This won't do at all."

"What seems to be the difficulty? I've never known a simple lock to prove much of an impediment to you."

"If only this were a simple lock," he replied. "It's the latest model Chubb and it requires a key. No, old friend, I'm afraid we won't be entering the building this way."

"What about the rear door? It's much smaller; perhaps we could force our way in."

We walked around to the back where Holmes examined both the door and lock. "It's not a Chubb lock, but it's a sturdy one," he said as he focused his lantern upon the rear door. "I'll give it a try," he said as he extracted a thin leather case from his inside pocket. "Hold the lantern steady like a good fellow."

Holmes then set to work, gently probing the inner workings of the mechanism with his picks. Although it seemed as though he had been working at it for hours, a few minutes later the lock popped open. We eased the door ajar and slipped silently inside. We were standing in some sort of enclosed foyer with a door at the other end.

"Let's hope that's not locked as well," I said. We crept the eight or ten feet and I noticed the atmosphere inside had become very close. Cupping his hands to my ear, Holmes whispered, "Look at the floor, Watson."

Following his finger in the near-darkness, I gazed down where I discerned a faint line of light at the very bottom of the door. Holmes knelt down and peered through the keyhole. "My word," I heard him exclaim under his breath. Turning back to me, he whispered, "I think the room is empty, but have your pistol at the ready just in case." In the darkness, Holmes hadn't noticed that I'd been holding my revolver in one hand and the dark lantern in the other, ever since he had begun to work on the lock.

He gently eased open the door a crack and after a furtive glance he opened it wider. I wasn't quite sure what to make of what I saw before me. I just knew that I had never seen anything like it before.

In the middle of the room stood a large canvas tent. Although there appeared to be no one present, the tent was brightly illuminated from the inside while the rest of the room remained in semi-darkness. On the floor in front of the tent stood a number of metal cylinders – perhaps forty of them – with wire connections at the top of several of them.

"Batteries," whispered Holmes. "Obviously they are providing the illumination inside the tent." Pointing to the array, he added, "And they seem to have plenty of spares."

"What do you suppose this is all about?" I asked my friend.

Pulling back one of the flaps from the entrance to the tent, he peered cautiously inside and then I heard him chuckle. "Just as I suspected, I think we are looking at some sort of greenhouse," he stated.

"A greenhouse? Indoors, inside a tent, on a dock? You can't be serious!"

As he pulled the flap back wider, I took in the contents of the tent. On the floor, I saw four large plant boxes. In each, there grew shafts of wheat perhaps three fight high. Looking about, I noticed that two sides of the tent featured an array of electric lights while the other two were illuminated by similar lights but with some sort of prism in front of the bulbs.

"What do you make of this Holmes?"

"I believe they are growing four different types of wheat blight spores which at some point will soon be tested on fields in England and perhaps elsewhere – if they haven't been already."

"What about the different lights?"

"I'm inclined to think these two beds," he said indicating the pair to our left, "are being subjected to regular light while those," he said pointing first to the remaining beds and then the prisms, "are being grown under ultraviolet light. I'm sure they are trying to increase the yield, hence the different types of illumination."

By now we were inside the tent and the flap had fallen closed behind us. It had been quite warm in the warehouse when we had entered and even warmer inside the tent – probably to simulate the heat of a summer sun, I thought. Looking around, I then noticed a quartet of strange-looking machines I didn't recognize, sitting on the floor. All had four large, long light bulbs in front of them arrayed like a fan and each was facing a bed of wheat.

"What are those, Holmes?"

"They would be one of Mr. Edison's newer inventions – portable electric heaters," he replied.

"My word, I had no idea," I said.

"Yes, I believe he invented the heater just a few short years after his much-heralded light bulb."

"Given they are so new, they must be quite expensive, so it would seem they have spared no expense in bringing this plot to fruition."

Holmes gave me a rather strange look, and it was only then I realized the poor taste of my unintended pun.

"Indeed," he replied. "Everything in this room is the latest technology and it's all powered by an array of batteries, no doubt procured from the nearby Electrical Power Storage Co."

"But wouldn't that attract a great deal of attention – delivering batteries on a regular basis to an empty warehouse?"

"I'm certain whoever is behind this found a way to cover his tracks."

It had been quite warm and humid when we entered the warehouse, but the temperature seemed to have risen since our arrival. I said to Holmes, who was busy examining the plants, "Has it got hotter in here, or am I imagining things?"

All of a sudden, there was a bright flash as one side of the canvas tent erupted in flame. The blaze quickly consumed the rest of the fragile structure and as we made our way back to the door, Holmes said, "We must have tripped some sort of booby-trap when we entered."

I reached for the doorknob and twisted it, but it had locked. As I looked around me, I could see the flames spreading rapidly. I searched the room for another exit but my efforts were fruitless. As the smoke grew thicker, I suddenly realized Holmes was no longer behind me. As I peered through the haze, I could just see him kneeling by one of the flower boxes. After a moment, he jumped up, sprinted past me and threw his entire body against one of the windows. Although the safety glass gave somewhat, the wire helped it remain intact.

"Stand aside, Holmes," I bellowed, and I then emptied my revolver into the glass spacing the holes as best I could. While I was firing, Holmes had seized one of the metal batteries from the floor and together we used it as a battering ram and made a large hole in the center of the pane. Using his coat to cover his hands, Holmes then proceeded to pry loose a large shard of glass. I did the same and a moment later we were breathing the fetid air of the Thames which had never tasted so sweet.

We stepped back and watched helplessly as the fire rapidly consumed the building. In the distance, I could hear shouts of "Fire! Fire!" I knew the fire brigade would never get here in time.

We melted into the shadows of a nearby warehouse and watched as a company of men arrived in a steam-powered fire engine some fifteen minutes later. By that time, the warehouse had been almost totally destroyed – the building having collapsed in on itself – and the men devoted the bulk of their energies to hosing down nearby buildings lest a stray ember cause another conflagration.

Later, as we made our way back to Baker Street on foot, I said to Holmes, "Do you think that trap was set for us?"

"I'm inclined to doubt it," he replied. "They had no way of knowing we would pay them a nocturnal visit. No, I believe when we entered we tripped an alarm of some sort. Those aware of it would disarm or deactivate it. It was our failure to do so that resulted in the blaze.

"However, it reinforces the idea that we are up against an adversary to whom human life means little. It was worth it to him to burn down a building, and the people and crops inside – not to mention the rather expensive machinery – rather than run the risk of discovery."

"My word, Holmes, that is dastardly. Anyone could have been trapped in there."

"Yes, it was fortunate that you had brought your pistol. The bullets helped weaken that wire glass."

"What will they do next?"

"That's impossible to say, but I think it is high time I had a rather lengthy conversation with my brother. For all his claims of ignorance, I am certain he must know more about this than he has told us. Perhaps he has made some progress of his own."

Holmes than lapsed into silence for the rest of our trek, and I realised he was attempting to unravel a problem about which he knew precious little. At one point, we might have been able to ride home as we encountered a lonely cab on Northumberland Avenue, When I suggested we hire the hansom, Holmes muttered, "If it's all the same to you, I'd rather walk." Although my leg had begun to bother me after a long day filled with walking, I soldiered on in silence in case Holmes should need a sounding board.

As we neared Piccadilly, I recalled that during the case I had titled "The Adventure of the Copper Beeches," Holmes had exclaimed in frustration, "Data! Data! I cannot make bricks without clay."

I carefully considered our situation and wondered, given the lack of data whence the "clay" might come. However, I had long maintained an implicit, unwavering faith in my friend and he had yet to fail me. Feeling a bit better, I noticed that we had just turned onto Baker Street. "Perhaps tomorrow," I thought, with just a hint of optimism.

Chapter Seven

I slept late the next morning and came down to find Holmes sitting at his microscope staring intently at a slide he had obviously prepared. So engrossed was he that I wasn't certain he had even heard me descend the stairs. When I picked up the papers, I saw the fire in the warehouse had made it into all of the dailies. "Holmes, were you able to glean anything from the papers about the blaze?"

He looked up from the microscope and shook his head. "By all accounts, it was a vacant warehouse, that had been rented to a French firm several months ago."

"That sounds promising. Can you not investigate that business?"

"I'm certain the papers filed were false, and that no such company as *Le Syndicat des Céréales* even exists. Still I will make inquiries because in this case we must leave no stone unturned."

"Have you written to Mycroft?"

"I sent a telegram earlier this morning and am awaiting a reply. By the way, Watson, did anything strike you as unusual about the wheat we saw growing in that warehouse?"

"I'm afraid my experience with farming and various strains of wheat is rather limited. Why? Did you notice something out of the ordinary?"

"Here, take a look for yourself and tell me what you see."

I gazed through the microscope and after adjusting the focus, I could readily discern the first two samples were quite similar while the third appeared distinctly different. After I had said so to Holmes, he replied "Excellent. We'll make a botanist of you yet, old man."

He continued, "The first two specimens are spelt wheat, which has been cultivated in Germany for centuries while the third sample, the lighter one, is durum wheat which is a popular crop here in the England."

"I can see where this is going, but I can't believe you risked your life in a fire in order to obtain some wheat samples."

"I needed to be certain that they were the same strain and now I am."

"And now that you know they are the same how does that help us?"

"My fear was that they were developing a variety of blights, but since we now have a sample from a field that matches one being grown in a greenhouse, I think we can safely conclude that there is but one blight that affects various varieties of wheat. In a sense, Watson, we now know our enemy, and perhaps Mycroft's minions can discover an anti-fungal for this one type of blight instead of pursuing fruitless endeavours and trying to protect us against threats that do not exist – at least not yet." The last four words were uttered with a certain terseness that I had come to recognize in Holmes's voice, and I knew it did not bode well for our enemies.

As he continued at his chemistry table, I returned to my breakfast which had cooled somewhat during our discussion. I also continued my perusal of the papers when I came across a small article buried deep on a page of financial news within *The Times*.

"I say, Holmes, did you see this piece in the paper about a certain German industrialist who is seeking to acquire a seat on the London Stock Exchange?"

"I seldom read the financial news. Did I miss something of import?"

"Don't you find it rather odd that a German is trying to secure a position that will allow him to trade on the market and most certainly provide entree into the London Produce Clearing House?"

"By Jove, Watson, I think you may be onto something. Such a seat would allow him clearing services for futures contracts in coffee, sugar, and other soft commodities…"

"Such as wheat," I finished the sentence for him.

"Does it provide a name?" Holmes inquired.

"Unfortunately, no."

"That's easily found out – either through Pike or my brother. Speaking of whom, if he hasn't responded by noon, I think we'll join him for lunch at the Diogenes Club. Would you care to accompany me?"

Of course, I agreed, and I must admit that the rest of the morning seemed an eternity. We finally had what appeared to be a fresh, new lead, yet Holmes remained preoccupied with his experiments and carried on as though nothing of import had occurred.

I tried a dozen different things to busy my mind but to no avail. Finally, at about half twelve, Holmes looked up, glanced at his watch, and said, "Unless I am much mistaken, my brother should be rising from his desk right about now and considering his options for lunch. If we hurry and catch a cab, I would imagine we can meet on the steps of the club before he has even had time to enter."

"Is Mycroft that much a creature of habit that you can anticipate his schedule to the very minute?"

"Unless something totally unexpected and unprecedented should arise, Mycroft is the most predictable man I know."

We found a cab without issue and perhaps twenty minutes later, we were standing outside the Diogenes Club. Holmes pointed up the street to his brother who was ambling towards us at a leisurely pace and said, "See, here he comes now."

Although Mycroft had seen us as well, he made no effort to increase his speed and when he finally did arrive, he looked at Holmes and said, "I rather expected to find you here."

"Indeed?" replied Holmes just a bit testily. "Perhaps if you had replied to my telegram, you'd have known rather than merely expected."

"Sherlock, please. I have had a most trying morning, and I do apologize for not replying. Believe me, I would have written you this afternoon as soon as things have sorted themselves out."

"What has happened?"

Glancing about, Mycroft said, "Not now – and certainly not here."

We entered and made our way to the Stranger's Room. I wondered how many more times I would find myself here before the case was brought to a resolution.

I was last to enter and was rather surprised to find another man inside, apparently waiting for us. He was quite thin, perhaps nine stone, and although he was about my height, he appeared taller because of his slender frame. He had thick brown hair with a full beard and mustache.

No sooner had the door closed behind us, then Mycroft said, "Ah, Steven, thank you for taking the time to meet us." Turning to Holmes and me, Mycroft said, "This is Dr. Steven Smith, one of the leading botanists in the country. I am sure you can guess why I invited him here."

After we had exchanged pleasantries, Holmes said, "Are you any relation to Worthington G. Smith, the illustrator and plant pathologist?"

Steven Smith smiled and said, "I get asked that question quite often and my standard answer is 'Perhaps.' As you might expect, there are a great number of Smiths running around these days."

"True, but how many can claim to be rather prominent botanists?" countered Holmes.

"Prominent, Mr. Holmes?" replied Smith, "Why on Earth would you think that?"

Holmes smiled at Smith and then he said, "Because Mycroft surrounds himself with only the top people in their fields." He then paused letting the obvious implication sink in.

"Touché, Sherlock!" exclaimed Mycroft, as there was a knock on the door. "Come," he said, and a young man wheeled in a trolley piled high with various sandwiches. He left and returned a moment later with a similar cart laden with an assortment of beverages. When the man had departed,

Mycroft said, "I took the liberty of ordering ahead for everyone."

After we had got settled with our food and drink, Mycroft said, "Here is what we know thus far." He then recapped what Holmes had seen at the farm he had visited for Smith as well as what the two of us had discovered in the warehouse. He then informed us that it was Smith in the company of another agent who had investigated the other farm in the Cotswolds. He explained that when Smith arrived, the farm was deserted.

"And the fields?" inquired Holmes.

"They looked as though they had suffered through a plague. The wheat had been largely shriveled and what little survived was of such poor quality as to render it worthless," explained Smith. "It was quite obvious that it had been planted, tended and then for whatever reason abandoned."

"Did you take samples?" asked Holmes.

"We were only able to collect a few, but enough to tell us the infection was caused by a blight called *Fusarium graminearum.*"

"Isn't that exactly the same as the sample my brother provided from the farm near Manchester?" asked Mycroft.

"It is," replied Smith.

"And what type of wheat was infected in the Cotswolds?" asked Holmes.

"It was a type of hard wheat that had apparently been cross-bred with durum wheat."

"And were both affected equally by the disease?"

"Where are you going with this, Sherlock?" asked Mycroft.

"You will see soon enough," my friend replied. Turning back to Smith, he repeated the question, "And were both affected equally by the disease?"

"They were," replied Smith.

"Excellent," replied Holmes.

"Excellent?" queried Mycroft. "How can any threat to the economy of the Empire, and perhaps the world, ever be described as 'Excellent'?"

And then it hit me: "You need to develop only one fungicide. With any luck, it will kill the blight without harming the wheat plants."

"Is such a thing possible?" Mycroft asked Smith.

"Theoretically, it might be possible" he replied, choosing his words carefully. "Of course we'd have to test it on the blight being employed and see what effects both the blight and the wheat exhibit as a result of the exposure."

"Do you have other samples of the blight, perhaps of a different strain?" asked Mycroft.

"Unfortunately not," replied Smith. "When the farmer returned and saw what had transpired in his fields, he took great pains to clear the land, so we were lucky to get away with any at all."

"I may be able to help," said Holmes, pulling two envelopes from his inner jacket pocket. "These are a few additional samples taken from the farm near Manchester while these were collected at the warehouse that burned down on the Isle of Dogs."

"That's marvelous," exclaimed Smith. "I shall bring them back to the lab, and my team and I will begin to study them and see if we can devise some sort of anti-fungal immediately."

"Do be careful," cautioned Holmes. "Those are the last samples we have, and the chances of obtaining any others are slim at best."

"You have my word, Mr. Holmes." With that he snatched his hat from the rack and was out the door.

"He's quite a brilliant fellow," said Mycroft, "and for him the words King and Country are far more than just a phrase. Of course, developing an anti-fungal is just the beginning," he continued, "we'll have to devise a delivery system – all the while trying to keep it from the public and the press so as to avoid a national panic."

"My word," I exclaimed. "Were the public to learn of the threat, there would be mass panic and hoarding and prices would soar to record highs."

"All that can be avoided," interjected Holmes, "if we can locate the mastermind behind this plot and stop him in his tracks."

"Locating ne'er-do-wells is rather your stock in trade, isn't it?" asked Mycroft.

"To a degree," replied my friend. "But in order to ply my trade effectively, I need information."

"Well, I'm still quite taken with the notion that you regard my specialty as omniscience, so feel free to ask anything."

"I never actually said that," replied my friend a bit testily, casting a baleful glance in my direction.

And before the exchange could grow any more tense, I interjected, saying, "I might have taken some liberties with the intent of your brother's speech, Mycroft, but rest assured, he does admire your considerable gifts."

Holmes shot me another look, but Mycroft seemed mollified, and he repeated in a somewhat more subdued tone, "How can I help?"

"There was a small article in the paper this morning about a German industrialist who is seeking to secure a seat on the London Stock Exchange. Can you tell me anything about the man in question?"

"I know his name – Robert X. Edelman – although I shouldn't be surprised if he has Anglicized his name given our rather tense relations with the Kaiser."

"So you think his real name might be Rupert Edelmann?" said Holmes, giving the proper pronunciation of the last syllable by softening the a.

"It's quite possible," replied Mycroft. "I can have my people look into him if you like."

"If your people," said Holmes, underscoring the last two words, "could put together some background material on him that would be helpful. But it must be done quite carefully so as not to arouse suspicion."

"Of course," replied Mycroft. "Is there anything else?"

"Do you happen to have any idea where I might find him?"

"I believe he has rented a townhouse in Westminster, not too far from the German Embassy at Prussia House on Carlton House Terrace."

"So he's staying close to the embassy but not actually in it?"

"Sherlock, take care," cautioned Mycroft, "even my reach is limited in certain areas."

Ignoring his brother, Holmes rose to his feet and said, "Come, Watson, there's work to be done,"

I quickly bolted down the rest of my sandwich, bid Mycroft farewell and followed Holmes out the door. When we had reached the pavement, I said to him, "I shudder to ask, but what exactly are you thinking?"

"That it's far easier to burgle a private residence – something with which you and I have some small degree of experience – than it is to break into an embassy."

"And far less dangerous," I added. I had to smile in spite of myself, as I thought back to the many times Holmes and I had played fast and loose with the legal code over the years. Being on the wrong side of the law wasn't exactly a new experience.

"We have been fortunate thus far," I said. "I pray that our luck continues."

"Yes," chuckled Holmes, "hopefully things will go smoothly this time. After all," he added, "practice does make perfect."

I had no idea at the time how prophetic my friend's words would prove to be.

Chapter Eight

After we had made our way back to Baker Street, Holmes quickly despatched the boy in buttons with a telegram and then disappeared into his room. He emerged perhaps twenty minutes later looking the part of a prosperous banker or solicitor. Padding had given my normally slim friend a rather obvious paunch. He had also concealed his appearance with a full beard and muttonchop sideburns – both of which were of a bright red hue – and a pair of tinted wire-rimmed glasses. Although the alterations may sound slight, when taken as a whole they completely altered his appearance.

"I say, old man, what are you about?"

"I plan to conduct a little reconnaissance of Herr Edelman's townhouse."

"Can I be of any assistance?"

"Not at the moment," and having made that pronouncement, he wandered over to his bookshelf, extracted one of his commonplace books, took a seat by the window and proceeded to pore over its contents. Admittedly, I found his behaviour rather unusual, even a bit unsettling, but I said nothing.

Perhaps a half hour later, I heard the front bell ring and a minute or two after that there was a soft tapping on the door. I opened it and was surprised to find Serene Adler standing there. "Please come in, my dear. It is so nice to see you again."

She entered the room, glanced at Holmes who had risen at her entrance, took in the rest of her surroundings and then turned to me with a rather surprised look on her face. "I am so sorry to have disturbed you, Dr. Watson. I only just returned to my hotel where I found a wire from Mr. Holmes waiting for me. He asked that I meet him here as soon as possible, so I jumped into a cab and here I am. And it appears that Mr. Holmes has either been delayed or he or someone else is playing a cruel prank on me."

"I would never be so unkind as to do such a thing," uttered Holmes.

I could see that Miss Adler was nonplussed, but she quickly recovered her composure and said, "I think that disguise, subtle as it may be, might have deceived even my sister, for it certainly fooled me."

After acknowledging the compliment, Holmes said, "I need to get a close look at a certain townhouse in Westminster. I have devised a plan to get us inside, but it's one more easily carried out by a couple than by two men. Should we be successful, I also want the inhabitants of the house to have no idea that they have been visited by Sherlock Holmes."

"We aren't going to do anything illegal, are we?" she asked.

"Not at all," replied Holmes.

"No, that will come later," I thought, but I remained silent.

"It's just a harmless deception so that I can get the lie of the land, if you will. You will be in no danger – either from the law or anything or anyone else, I promise," said Holmes.

"Do I have to do anything besides walk with you?"

"Do you think you can faint on cue?" asked Holmes, as he took her arm and escorted her towards the door.

I never did hear her answer, but when Holmes finally returned some three hours later, I could tell by the smile on his face that things had gone well.

"Where is Miss Adler?" I questioned.

"She asked me to leave her off at her hotel as she had a previous engagement for dinner and needed time to change."

Having answered my question, Holmes headed for his bedroom.

"And was your scheme successful?"

"Just let me remove this makeup, and I shall answer all your questions," he said.

Ten minutes later, he emerged looking much like his usual self. The beard, muttonchops and glasses had vanished as had the extra avoirdupois. Holmes headed for the sideboard and poured himself a sherry. "Care to join me?" he asked, and when I nodded, he filled a second glass for me.

Taking his usual seat, he began the machinations of preparing his pipe. I was glad to see that he had selected his old black pipe, so I waited patiently. I knew he was savoring the moment, so I let him enjoy it. Finally, he broke the silence, "You should have seen her, Watson! She was magnificent! She is as fine an actress as her sister."

"As you have so often instructed your clients, please begin at the beginning – and omit no detail, no matter how insignificant it may seem," I said.

Having been hoisted by his own petard, he smiled ruefully and said, "I suppose I deserved that."

After taking a sip of sherry, he began, "We took a cab to St. James Square and then proceeded on foot. I pretended to be looking for a house to purchase and inquired of several liveried servants if they knew of any. As you might expect, there is nothing available. From what little I could gather Edelman is staying at 4 Carlton House Terrace, which was the home of the German Embassy until quite recently when it was moved to 9 Carlton House Terrace.

"While there were two guards standing outside the embassy, I noticed no such protection at Number 4. When Miss Adler did swoon on our second pass in front of the house, I had her lean on my shoulder and feign unconsciousness while I rang the bell.

"As we waited, I happened to notice the front door of Number 4 is secured with a new Chubb lock; it appears identical to the one on the warehouse. Eventually, the portal swung open to reveal a hulking brute of a man whose name is Fritz. Although he was dressed like a butler, it was obvious he was wearing a shoulder holster under his jacket, and given his bearing and mannerisms he either was – or still is – a member of the Kaiser's army.

"At any rate, I asked if a doctor were present, and he said 'Nein.' So although he understood English, he answered in his native tongue. I then asked if he would summon a cab for us. Despite his rather loutish appearance, he was a most agreeable fellow; unfortunately, rather than leave us alone, he called a young lad from the street and instructed him in a mix of German and English to procure a dogcart for us. After the lad had departed, Miss Adler then appeared to come round and in a whisper of a voice requested water. While Fritz was fetching that, I was able to inspect the windows. They are quite new and made of steel. As you might expect, they boast reinforced glass. In short, the house is a veritable fortress. The only good thing is there are no dogs as far as I can tell."

"You could always try the direct approach and invent some pretext for a meeting. Mycroft might be of assistance with that particular endeavour."

"I shall turn to Mycroft for assistance only as a last resort. Come, old friend, we have solved problems far more vexing than a heavily fortified home." Having made that pronouncement, he threw himself into his chair, drew up his knees and lapsed into an all-too-familiar silence.

"Did you see any other guards inside during your visit?"

Holmes merely grunted, and I took his answer, such as it was, to be a negative.

"You could always have the Irregulars watch the house and let you know as soon as he leaves." Apparently this possibility had already crossed his mind, for I didn't even get so much as a grunt by way of reply. Having been rebuffed twice, I decided to leave Holmes to his own devices.

I informed Mrs. Hudson that I would have supper at my club. I also told her that Holmes was in one of his moods and that she should save herself the trouble of cooking a full dinner and just bring up some soup or sandwiches and coffee. She thanked me for my consideration, and I then made my way to my club. Once there, I treated myself to an excellent veal chop for dinner, complemented by a delightful Zinfandel. To top off the evening, I proceeded to recoup the price of my meal by taking several matches of snooker from Thurston. All in all, it turned out to be a most enjoyable evening.

When I returned home, I expected to find Holmes much as I had left him, but I was surprised to discover the flat empty and even more stunned to see that he had consumed one of the sandwiches Mrs. Hudson had prepared for him. Not wanting the other to go to waste, I decided to eat it myself, and I had just finished when the door opened and in strode Holmes looking quite pleased with himself.

He looked at me, smiled and said, "I cannot believe that I couldn't see it. The answer was right there in front of me the entire time."

"May I assume you have devised a safe way to search Herr Edelman's home."

"You may indeed, old friend, and the answer is simplicity itself. By the way, I assume you had a profitable evening at your club. Which was it? Cards or billiards?"

"You're the detective, you tell me."

"Billiards," he pronounced and as I started to smile he corrected himself, "No, not billiards – snooker."

"How the devil could you have known that?"

"There's just the slightest hint of blue on the knuckle of your index finger which you often place there to make the cue slide more smoothly."

I gazed at my left hand and was stunned to see the faint remnants of the chalk. Undaunted, I continued, "And why snooker instead of billiards?"

"Simplicity itself!" he pronounced. "Your waistcoat has a rather pronounced indentation just below the pocket. That occurs from your having to reach to make shots on the larger snooker table. On those occasions when I know you have played billiards, your waistcoat has remained uncreased."

In an effort to mitigate my embarrassment, I decided to change the topic. "I'd like to hear about the plan you've devised."

Holmes then proceeded to outline his plan, and truth be told, if one or two things fell his way, the plan was practically foolproof – or so it seemed at the time.

The next morning I came down to breakfast around 9 o'clock. Mrs. Hudson informed me that Holmes had risen early and left perhaps an hour before. I could only assume that he was out attempting to line up the pieces he would employ in his strategem.

When I returned home for lunch and found Holmes sitting at the table, I decided to beard the lion in his den. "I assume your plan proceeds apace."

"It does," he offered.

"What exactly is it that you are hoping to find?"

"Anything that might tie Edelman to any of the farms or the warehouse. Perhaps he'll be kind enough to leave papers linking him to the blight – although I'm inclined to doubt that."

"Don't you think anything like that would be under lock and key, if it is there it all? Perhaps he carries such papers with him at all times or perhaps they are kept someplace else entirely. In which case, this is all just a wild goose chase."

"Valid points all, Watson. However, we must begin somewhere, and his library seems like a logical spot."

"What if they are being kept down the street in the German Embassy? Surely, you're not considering trying to break in there. It might be considered an act of espionage and you could be shot."

"Let's cross that bridge when we come to it. Right now, I need to focus my attention on 4 Carlton House Terrace and the problems it presents. I have the Irregulars watching the house day and night so that we may learn the routines of the occupants. Their information may well prove to be crucial."

"Anything else I should know?"

"I've decided to ask Mycroft to make a few discreet inquiries for me – specifically as to the presence of a safe and if so, what make and model."

"Can he do that?"

"Never underestimate the reach of my brother. Quite frankly, I should imagine it is being done as we speak. I impressed upon him the need to obtain this information with all due haste. I am certain he will not let me down."

Sensing an opening, I asked, "What else did you request of your brother?"

"Merely that Herr Edelman be invited to a soiree this Friday evening at the home of Jonathan Knoxley."

"Who just happens to sit on the board of the London Stock Exchange," I added.

"As you know, I don't believe in coincidences but that certainly seems to be one," Holmes added dryly.

"Why Friday? If time is of the essence as you suggest, why not tomorrow night?"

"Because I need a few days to ascertain the routines of those residing at Number 4. Also, I've become convinced nothing will happen to the English crops until Edelman has secured that seat."

"Pray tell, how did you arrive at that conclusion?"

"Human nature, my friend. Edelman wants to destroy the English economy; I think we can agree on that."

"That would seem to be his plan."

"Unfortunately, for him, there's no telling how other nations might react. Canada would most certainly come to our aid and increase their production as might the Americans, who took in hundreds of thousands of Irish, perhaps more than a million souls, during the famine.

"No, Edelman needs to be in a position to control at least some of that – not to mention turning a tidy profit at the same time – which he cannot do unless he secures that coveted seat that will allow him to trade in futures."

"My word, he is a cad," and then a thought struck me. "How long have you been planning this?"

"I started the moment we learned of Edelman's address."

"I should have expected as much."

After he finished his lunch, Holmes disappeared into his bedroom and emerged a few minutes later in one of his favorite disguises, that of a Bobby. He had donned a dark blue frock coat with a high collar and shiny brass buttons. He had added light-colored trousers and a peaked cap with a brim. He also sported a leather belt with a truncheon. To complete the ensemble, he had donned a thick black beard and side-whiskers.

"My word, Holmes, you look quite dashing in that get-up. What are you about?"

"I want to get another look at Number 4 – from as many angles as possible this time. Quite possibly there are a few chinks in the armour which we can turn to our advantage. Also, who would suspect an officer of the law of being up to any chicanery? Just as they have done, Watson, I'm hiding in plain sight."

After he had departed, I marveled at his boundless energy and admired his courage. Too many times, we had found ourselves confronting what appeared to be innocent situations only to have them suddenly go sideways – sometimes with devastating results. I could only hope this wasn't one of those times.

Chapter Nine

Holmes returned early that evening. After he had removed his disguise and enjoyed his dinner, which Mrs. Hudson had kept warm for him, I finally asked, "Did you learn anything from your excursion?"

"I learned that Mr. Edelman is approximately my height, though somewhat heavier than I. He sports a full beard and mustache and has a certain innate intelligence, a natural cunning if you will. Were he not such a villain, I could almost admire the fellow."

"Did you speak to him, Holmes? It certainly sounds as though you did."

"Yes, I was investigating the rear of the house – you'll be happy to know there is no Chubb lock on the door to the kitchen. I had just finished my examination and was returning to the street when Edelman's coach pulled up. As he stepped down, he gazed at me warily and asked, "Is something amiss, Constable?"

"'No sir,' I replied. 'I was chasin' a young hooligan suspected of thievin' from the kitchen of the Reform Club on Pall Mall. I followed him into your rear yard but he give me the slip when he jumped over the fence. I'm not as young as I used to be, I guess.'

"'Perhaps he was desperately hungry,' said Edelman 'Hunger will drive a man – or a boy – to desperation.'

"I'm sure you're right, sir, but that's still no excuse for breakin' the law."

"'You would know best there, Constable,' he said. 'Thank you.' And with that he walked into the house, followed closely by Fritz, the 'butler,' who now appears to be something more than just a servant. You may recall I encountered Fritz during my foray with Miss Adler."

"Was Fritz armed, Holmes?"

"I am almost certain that he was. He certainly appeared to be wearing a shoulder holster which he apparently favours. At any rate, it's good to know that Fritz travels with Edelman. Let's hope they stick to form Friday evening."

The next few days were relatively uneventful. As you might expect, Holmes was in and out of Baker Street at all hours, and when he was home, he received regular reports from the Irregulars who were keeping watch on the house on Carlton House Terrace.

Late Friday afternoon, Holmes received another report from a youngster called Jeb. "Same as always, Mr. 'Olmes. If the Edelman fella goes out, the other bloke always goes with 'im."

After thanking the lad, Holmes looked at me, smiled and said, "Things could not have gone better if I had planned them myself."

"Oh?"

"There are no live-in servants at Number 4. The maids go home at six, and the cook and butler depart shortly after dinner."

"You mean there's just Edelman and Fritz in that huge house?"

"It would appear so. Best of all, the back lock remains unchanged."

"How do you know that?"

"One of the Irregulars has been doing odd jobs there in exchange for food. I asked him to pay particular attention to the lock, and according to his report, and I quote, 'Same ol' lock.' With any luck we'll be inside in no time and have an opportunity to give the place a good once over without fear of interruption."

After dinner, Holmes read while I began compiling my notes on this case. I like to record things while they are fresh in my mind. Around nine o'clock, he rose and said, "You might want to change into dark clothing, and I'd suggest wearing a pair of rubber-soled shoes."

Twenty minutes later, sporting a navy coat and dark trousers, I rejoined Holmes, who was similarly attired, in the sitting room. "You have your revolver, I trust?"

I nodded and patted my pocket. "Good, I have the dark lantern," he said, holding it up. "Now, let us be about my brother's business." We descended the stairs and left through the tradesmen's entrance. I looked at Holmes and he replied, "Just in case we are being watched."

We cut through the alley and emerged onto Park Lane, which runs parallel to Baker Street. As we walked, the city seemed unusually quiet for a pleasant Friday evening. There were several couples taking in the night air at Berkeley Square but far fewer than I might have expected on such a delightful evening. We walked down Carlton Gardens, and near the end we encountered Giggy, one of the Irregulars, at the corner of Carlton Terrace. The lad had ensconced himself behind a boxwood hedge in an effort to remain undetected.

"The toff and the big fella left a while ago, Mr. 'Olmes in a big fancy carriage. The house is dark, the curtains are drawn, and no one's come in or gone out."

"Excellent, Giggy. You have your instructions. Now stay sharp and if you see the carriage return or anyone about to enter the house, you know what to do."

"Yes, sir," the lad replied, holding up a police whistle. Holmes handed the lad a few coins and said, "Dr. Watson and I are counting on you."

"I won't let you down, sir," he promised earnestly.

We then made our way down another alley and after climbing a fence, we found ourselves in the garden behind Number 4. Holmes moved to the door and extracted the slim leather case, which held his lock picks. I lit the dark lantern. He grunted in satisfaction as he manoeuvered the tumblers, and in less than a minute the door gave way to his ministrations.

We stood there in silence, listening for any sound that might indicate the presence of someone in the house, but none was forthcoming.

After a moment, we made our way through the kitchen and down a hall that appeared to feature portraits of various German noblemen and dignitaries – none was more prominently displayed than that of Kaiser Wilhelm II. Holmes moved with a quiet confidence and midway down the hall, he paused and tried a door on his left. "How do you know where things are if you never got beyond the waiting room?" I asked.

"Mycroft was kind enough to provide a set of blueprints. Unfortunately, he was no help with regard to a safe. Unless I am mistaken, this should be Edelman's library, which also doubles as his office."

We entered a spacious chamber which was almost pitch black. As the curtains were nearly closed, only a sliver of moonlight seeped in, but it provided little illumination. In the near darkness I could make out the outline of what I assumed was a massive desk. Behind it sat what I believed was a large chair with a very high back. From what little I could discern, it seemed more like a throne than anything else. Holmes turned his dark lantern on the walls on which had been hung several portraits and other paintings. I presume the daguerreotypes were either German aristocrats or relatives. One photo of a particularly striking woman caught my eye, and I was about to remark on it when Holmes stopped by one of the paintings, withdrew his lens and began to examine it.

"Is there a safe behind it?" I inquired.

Turning to me, he chuckled and said, "No, no safe, but I believe this is far more valuable than almost anything a safe could hold. Unless I am mistaken, this is an original portrait by Hans Holbein the Younger."

Suddenly a deep voice informed us, "You are not mistaken, Mr. Holmes. That is indeed a work by the younger Holbein. Look closely, and I am certain you will recognize the subject as Sir Thomas More, statesman and the author of the rather idealistic work, *Utopia*."

We had moved a few feet farther along the wall, when a bright lamp on the desk suddenly illuminated the two of us. As you might expect, for a moment I was startled by the unexpected brightness which had been focused on us – it was almost as if we had been captured by a small spotlight. As my eyes were adjusting, I heard Holmes say, "Herr Edelman, at long last we meet. Given your presence, I can only assume you were expecting us."

"You were supposed to be at a dinner party with Jonathan Knoxley, trying to secure a seat on the London Stock Exchange," I added.

"Knoxley is an idiot," replied Edelman. "He would no more invite me to dinner of his own volition than he would crash the market."

I started to say, "I don't understand…" but Edelman cut me off.

"You English are not the only ones who can play dress-up and pretend to be someone you are not. We Germans are equally adept at such ruses and games. Of course, Fritz had to go; no one could impersonate him. But a false beard – such as a constable might wear – and my driver could easily pass for me."

At that point, my eyes had regained their focus and I suddenly realized that Edelman, who was sitting in the chair behind the desk, was holding a large pistol in his right hand. He was smoking a cigarette and creating smoke rings when he exhaled. At that point my hand stole towards my pocket, but Edelman spotted the move and said, "I assume you are armed, Dr. Watson, so I would appreciate it if you kept your hands where I could see them at all times."

"What is it you want from us?" asked Holmes.

"I want to know what you have learned about my plan," said Edelman softly but firmly. "We can do this in one of two ways: You will answer all of my questions honestly and die a quick death with no pain whatsoever. Perhaps an overdose of morphine."

"And if we refuse to tell, you will torture us until we break and then you'll kill us anyway."

"Only after I have made you suffer a great deal more than necessary for wasting my time," he said with a smile.

"Well that's quite the dilemma. Thomas Hobson would be proud of you," said Holmes. Then changing tack completely, he inquired, "Before any unpleasantness begins, may I take another look at the Holbein?"

"Oh please, Mr. Holmes, I know exactly what you are planning and I can see what you are trying to do."

"Oh?"

"You are thinking there are two of you and only one of me and that if you step far enough away from Dr. Watson – and that would be just far enough to examine the painting – I may be able to get only one shot off before the other can attack me."

At that point, Edelman crushed out his cigarette in a rather large ashtray on the desk and then with his left hand he picked up a second pistol from the desk. It was immediately obvious that he was aiming the second pistol directly at me while the first remained focused on Holmes.

"I should warn you, Mr. Holmes, that I am ambidextrous and quite an accomplished marksman with either hand. So if you still wish to examine the painting by all means feel free to do so. I would never deny a dying man his last request."

"I have no doubt as to your ability as a marksman, so I will be quite careful when I examine the painting and equally circumspect in considering your offer.

"One other small indulgence, if I might?" asked Holmes.

"I will entertain your request, Mr. Holmes, but only because I too am such an admirer of the artist. What is it?"

"Could you pull back the curtains just a bit that I might have a bit more light with which to conduct my examination? And might I extract my lens from my pocket?"

"I was told you were a wise man, Mr. Holmes," said Edelman amiably. "But I beg you, please do not mistake my generosity for weakness. Dr. Watson, if you would be so kind as to stand a bit closer to Mr. Holmes while I draw back the curtains."

I did as he had requested, and Edelman then tucked one pistol in his waistband, and without ever taking his eyes or the gun off us, he reached behind him and drew back one of the heavy velvet curtains. "Now Mr. Holmes, your lens is in your right jacket pocket; you may remove it, but please do so with your left hand."

After taking out his glass, Holmes then moved to the painting and began to examine it quite carefully. His enthusiasm knew no bounds – "The brushwork is impeccable! Did you know that it was Erasmus who introduced Holbein to More? The attention to detail is stunning." As Holmes prattled on, one might have thought we were touring the Victoria and Albert Museum rather than being held at gunpoint by a madman.

After stepping back a bit to admire the painting as a whole, Holmes asked, "Is this the only Holbein in your possession?"

"Before I answer that, suppose you answer a question for me?"

"Certainly," replied Holmes amenably. "Do you mind if I smoke?"

"Help yourself," said Edelman, "would you like one of mine?"

"No thank you," replied Holmes, "I prefer my own brand."

"To each his own, Mr. Holmes. Now, if you would be so kind, what do you know, and more important, what does your brother, Mycroft, know of my plans?"

"You know about Mycroft?" I blurted out incredulously.

Edelman chuckled, "I will never understand that British sense of superiority. Do you think you operate in a vacuum, Doctor? We have spies just as you do, and they learn secrets just as yours do. The elder Holmes is well-known among certain segments of society in Europe although I daresay he has not achieved nearly the notoriety of his younger brother – thanks in large part to yourself." Turning to my friend, he continued, "Now, Mr. Holmes, I believe it is your turn."

"We first became aware of something amiss quite by accident."

All of a sudden, there was a loud pounding on the front door and a gruff voice bellowed, "Scotland Yard. Open up immediately, or we'll be forced to break in the door." At that moment, the light was extinguished, and we were once again in near darkness. "Hit the floor, Watson!" yelled Holmes as he grabbed my coat and pulled me to him. Suddenly, a single gunshot rang out and I heard it hit the wall where I had been.

I did as I was told and while lying there, I thought I heard faint footsteps. However, the pounding on the door continued unabated, and suddenly there was a loud crack as the frame gave way. I heard a man's voice ask, "Mr. Holmes, are you in there? Are you all right? I thought I heard a shot."

Next, I heard a boy's voice say, "I did exactly what you said, Mr. 'Olmes. When I saw the curtains open in the window, I fetched Constable Peters 'ere, and told him you and the doctor was in danger."

"What exactly happened here, Mr. Holmes?" the constable asked. "You two seem to be the only ones here."

"We are fine," replied Holmes who immediately set about turning on all the lights in the room. It was only then that I noticed a small door directly behind the chair.

"Holmes…" I began.

"I see it, Watson. That must be how he escaped." Turning to the police officer, he said, "Constable, would you be so kind as to rouse Inspector Lestrade and inform him he is needed here. You might tell him it is a matter of some urgency, so please take a cab."

"Yes, sir," replied the constable who then turned on his heel and exited the house post-haste.

Holmes then turned to the boy. "Giggy, you are to be commended. You followed my instructions to the letter and quite possibly saved Dr. Watson's life and my own."

"I was just doing me job," replied the lad, but I could see that he was thrilled with the praise my friend had heaped upon him.

Holmes looked at me and said, "I think such steadfastness warrants a bonus. What say you, Doctor?"

"I couldn't agree more."

Holmes then withdrew his pocketbook and extracted a £5 note and handed it to the boy. Giggy's eyes grew large but he said, "That's too much, Mr. 'Olmes."

"I think it's just right, Giggy, and the doctor agrees with me. So thank you again, and now hurry home, I'm certain your mum is worried."

The lad bowed awkwardly, thanked us profusely and then bolted from the room – he was even faster than the constable, I believe.

"Now what, Holmes?"

"While we wait for Lestrade, I suggest we search the place thoroughly." With that he set about rifling through the desk.

"What shall I do?"

"Take the dark lantern and see where that doorway takes you, but be careful. Edelman may still be lurking about. You have your pistol?"

I held up my hand.

"Keep it out and aimed in front of you, and if you feel threatened, shoot first, and we will sort it out later."

I went to the wall and opened the door. There was a narrow stairway cut in stone leading down to the cellar. The lantern provided precious little light, but not much was needed given the size of the passageway. I descended the stairway, all the while expecting Edelman to spring from some darkened niche. However, I soon discovered that there were no hidden crevices. After some ten feet, the passageway turned left. I placed the lamp on the floor and slid it out with my foot. Bending over, I then took a quick glance around the corner. All I could see were stone walls as the lamp's light was not powerful enough to illuminate the entire passage. I paused – my senses straining – but I could neither hear nor see anything.

Reaching into my pocket, I withdrew a few farthings which I threw into the darkness. When nothing happened, I picked up the lamp and turned the corner – holding the light far from my side. As I walked, I kept waiting for Edelman to jump out of the darkness. I had gone perhaps 60 feet when I came to a steel door. I tried the knob and found it was locked. I returned to Holmes, glad to be out of that passageway, and made my report.

"No doubt, the houses of this street share a common cellar storage area. The problem is the next house down is the German Embassy. We could certainly be arrested and quite possibly shot if we tried to force our way in there."

"Do you think Edelman will hole up there? Can we not arrest him when he leaves?"

"What shall we charge him with, old friend? We have no proof to link him to any crime, and to the best of my knowledge he has done nothing illegal.

"Also, we broke into his house, remember? He certainly has a right to defend himself and his property against intruders. The law would be against us there, I'm afraid. As for the rest of it, simply put, it would be our word against theirs because you can be certain Edelman would array a legion of men who will swear to whatever he tells them. Now, you go wait for Inspector Lestrade in the street. I'd like to search this room a bit more carefully – time permitting."

As I left the room, I saw Holmes holding up a map that had been on Edelman's desk. I wondered why Edelman had needed a map – and what information Holmes might have gleaned from it. When I reached the door, I turned back once more and saw my friend examining a small piece of red cloth through his lens. As you might expect, I had no idea what it might signify, but I was certain that sooner or later Holmes would discern its importance.

When I walked outside and looked up at the waxing moon, I was glad that it was a clear night. I wondered what might have happened had it been overcast, or worse raining, but again, I decided to let sleeping dogs lie.

After about ten minutes, Holmes joined me on the pavement, but before I could ask him if he had learned anything, Lestrade pulled up in a dogcart with Constable Peters sitting next to him. After instructing Peters to resume his duties, Lestrade turned to us and asked, "What have you got yourself into now, Mr. Holmes?"

Holmes quickly summarised the evening's events for Lestrade, omitting some of the more salient details such as the particular threat posed by the blight, and alluding to a matter of national security only in the vaguest of terms.

"I get the feeling you're not telling me everything," Lestrade said, "but then I've become rather used to that. What is it that you'd like me to do?"

Holmes asked him to station a man inside the home in the event Edelman should return through the cellar. "You might also post a constable outside – the front door is not secure. I have no doubt you can dismiss your men tomorrow morning when I'll have some of my Irregulars take over sentry duty."

"Having your boys replace my constables? Ordinarily, I'd be put out about that, but we are so short of men right now, I'll take whatever help I can get."

"Thank you, Inspector. Now, Watson, I think that's enough excitement for one evening. Perhaps a nightcap when we return home?"

"One drink and twenty questions," I thought to myself as we ambled off towards Baker Street. However, there was one burning question that I needed to have answered immediately. "When the light went out, why did you pull me towards you? How did you know Edelman would shoot at me and not at you?"

"Quite simple, really. I was standing directly in front of the Holbein."

Chapter Ten

After we had arrived home, Holmes went through the routine of changing into his dressing gown and charging his pipe. When he had lit the pipe – his old and oily black clay one – I looked at him and he nodded. So I went to the sideboard and poured two generous snifters of Armagnac. I handed one to Holmes and taking the other sat in my chair. After a moment's silence, I looked at him and said, "I'm sure you will tell me differently, but to these eyes, we appear to have lost ground tonight."

"Oh?" he replied.

"Edelman is in the wind, and we have no idea where he may surface."

"That is certainly true," replied Holmes.

I was stunned that he had agreed with my assessment, so I continued, "The plot to foil the economy proceeds, and we haven't any idea of how to stop it."

"We know how to stop it," he replied. "Locate their remaining test farm or farms and employ an anti-fungal that will destroy the blight before it can mature into spores. I believe Mycroft has his best men working on a solution to the problem as we speak."

"And if they cannot develop the anti-fungal that we need, then what?"

"We burn whatever crops they may have infected to the ground," he replied after taking another sip of brandy.

"First, we must find them which brings us back to where this discussion began. We have made no progress to speak of, have we?"

"That depends," he replied casually, and when I looked at him, I could see that his grey eyes were gleaming. "Do you believe men are creatures of habit?"

"More or less," I replied evasively, uncertain exactly where this conversation might be heading. "Why do you ask?"

"Edelman is German."

"Yes, I am well aware of that."

"He drinks only German wine and spirits."

"How could you know that?"

"While you were exploring the passageway, I was examining his sideboard. There I discovered two bottles of Gruner Silvaner, three bottles of Riesling and two more bottles of Zinfandel. Accompanying them were bottles of Bärenfang, Goldwasser and Kirschwasser. There was also a bottle of Rüdesheim cognac, a relatively new type of brandy that I'm told is quite good. Surprisingly, or perhaps not, there was not a single bottle of scotch or gin. Also, he smokes German cigarettes – which he rolls himself."

"And how does that help us?"

"Because he uses a brand of tobacco – Von Eichen – which is grown in Mulhern der Ruhr and is quite dear. You begin to see a pattern, I trust."

"I can see quite clearly that he prefers goods from his homeland."

"Exactly – *his* homeland! Have you ever seen a packet of Karos or Ivan Kerckhof cigarettes at Bradley's?"

"I can't say that I have."

"And yet he stocks a broad array of tobacco products…"

I cut Holmes off before he could finish. "You're going to find out what stores carry Von Eichen in London and hope that Edelman or one of his men shows up to buy his favorite tobacco."

"Exactly, old man. In point of fact, I know of only three merchants in town that might carry Von Eichen – although there may be others. However, we can visit all three tomorrow. After all, they don't have to send someone and take that risk, they can simply have them delivered to a bogus address or perhaps shipped to a post office box. It may take some time, but I believe we have discovered a thread that we can pull."

"How about the spirits? I know the wines are fairly common, but can we not do something with the various liquors he appears to prefer?"

"I'll make some inquiries when we are out tomorrow. The first thing I want to do in the morning is return to Number 4."

"Pray tell, why?"

"I want to examine the kitchen. Had I thought of it, I would have done so when we were there."

"And I presume you are hoping to find a pantry laden with German foodstuffs?"

"You have it exactly, old man." With that Holmes tossed back the last of his brandy, looked at me and said, "Get some sleep. We have a busy day tomorrow."

I nodded in agreement, finished my drink and bade Holmes good night. Sleep came quickly, and I awoke refreshed the next morning. I washed, dressed and went down to find Holmes sitting at the table, drinking coffee, reading the papers and smoking his first pipe of the day.

"Good morning, Watson. As soon as you've had some breakfast, we can be off."

I nodded and said, "Anything of note in *The Times*?"

"No, it appears to be a rather slow day. At this point, I'm convinced that no news is good news."

He then disappeared behind the broadsheet while I enjoyed my kippers, eggs and coffee. When I had finished, I said, "I'm ready when you are."

Holmes needed no urging and headed for the door immediately with me trailing in his wake.

Once outside, we hailed a cab and some fifteen minutes later, we found ourselves in front of 4 Carlton House Terrace. There was a constable on duty outside, who recognized us. "Mornin' Mr. Holmes. I was told you might drop by. Constable Peters is inside. No one has come back and the only ones who tried to get in were the cook and the maids. I told them they had the weekend off and to check with Inspector Lestrade before coming to work on Monday."

"Excellent, Constable. You have done well," Holmes said. We then entered the house, and my friend called out, "Hello."

"In the kitchen, Mr. Holmes," answered Peters. We proceeded down the hall and entered the kitchen to find Constable Peters reading a paper at the table.

"All is quiet, I presume," said Holmes.

"Indeed, it's been a long, dreary night."

"I think just one man need remain on duty. I'll leave it to you and the constable outside to decide who stays."

"Thank you, Mr. Holmes. As I said, it's been a tedious, boring night and I am quite famished and very tired." With that, he rose and headed for the front door.

No sooner had he left the kitchen than Holmes began examining the shelves of the pantry and pulling open the various cabinets. "Watson, see if there is a stone larder out back or a separate cellar where they might have kept meat."

I quickly discovered a second cellar that was cool and dry. Given the tubs that were now filled with water, I was pretty certain that they had ice delivered on a regular basis. In a smaller room, I discovered a smoker and a cabinet filled with various types of sausages.

When I returned to the kitchen and told Holmes of my discovery, he smiled that enigmatic smile I had seen so often. He told me the cabinets were filled with an array of German foodstuffs such as gooseberry jam, and various types of mustard, including mittelscharg. He also noted that while there was but a single loaf of white bread, there were three loves of pumpernickel.

"Now, Watson, consider everything we know and what emerges is a man who eschews English food and drink in favour of that which can be found in his homeland. Unfortunately, given the large number of Germans currently residing in London tracing foodstuffs may prove well-nigh impossible."

"So what are we to do?"

"Let's focus on the cigarettes. I want you to visit Bradley's when we leave here and see if he can suggest any other tobacconist where you might be able to purchase Von Eichen tobacco. Also inquire about any places that might carry German cigarettes – on the off-chance the tobacco is not readily available."

"And what will you be doing while I'm making those inquiries?"

"I have one other lead I wish to follow – a most tenuous one – and then I need to speak with Mycroft."

"Hopefully, he will have made some progress on the anti-fungal," I said.

With that Holmes and I exited Number 4. I hailed a cab that was passing and when I looked out, I saw Holmes had stopped and was speaking to the constable.

Perhaps fifteen minutes later, I was standing inside Bradley's. I have always enjoyed visiting my tobacconist, and today was no exception. The aromas of the various blends imbued the premises with a type of serene atmosphere that could be found in few other locations. The clerk, Frank, was familiar to me, and he asked, "What can I get for you today, Dr. Watson?"

After purchasing some cigarettes and pipe tobacco for both Holmes and myself, I asked, "Is Mr. Bradley in today?"

"Junior or Senior?" he replied.

Although I was more familiar with the younger Bradley, I was no stranger to his father, and in this case I thought Bradley Senior might be able to provide more information, so I said, "Senior."

"You're in luck," replied James. "He is in, but his son isn't. Just let me see if he is free."

A few minutes later, I was ushered into his office. The room was attractively decorated and the bookshelves on the walls were filled with all types of smoking implements – pipes, cigarette holders, cigar cutters and humidors. I could have spent hours just examining the various items, but I knew time was a factor.

In the center of the room was a gleaming partners desk, with matching green-shaded desk lamps and blotters. The elder Bradley rose when I entered, came around the desk and shook my hand. "Dr. Watson, it's so good to see you. I hope none of our products has displeased you."

"No, no, not at all," I said. "But I was wondering if you might be able to assist me with something."

"Are you working on a case with Mr. Holmes?" he asked.

Although I hated to lie to the man, I said, "No, nothing like that. I'm in the market for a very special gift. I don't believe you carry it, and I was wondering if you might be able to point me to someone who does?"

"It's tobacco-related, and we don't carry it?" he asked as though he thought I must be mistaken. "Pray tell, what exactly are you looking for?"

"I have a friend visiting from Austria and he is quite partial to Von Eichen tobacco. He constantly complains about both our own leaves as well as those grown in the Americas. He finds them too harsh."

"I can well believe that," replied Bradley. "Von Eichen tobacco is extremely mild – and that's one of the reasons we no longer carry it."

"One of the reasons?"

"Yes, the other is that it is quite expensive, so it wasn't selling terribly well."

Nodding, I said, "I understand. Still, I was wondering if you might know where I could purchase some. As I said it is a gift."

Bradley thought for a moment or two and then said, "The only three merchants I can think of off the top of my head that might carry it would be Robert Lewis on St. James Street, Fribourg & Treyer at 34 Haymarket, and Inderwicks, which is located in Wardour Street, Soho. I think Harrods might carry some of the Fox blends, but I can't be certain."

I thanked Bradley profusely and on my way back to Baker Street remonstrated with myself for not thinking of Lewis on my own. I had four places to consider although I didn't think a haughty German aristocrat such as Edelman would deign to shop in an English department store.

I found Holmes waiting for me when I entered the flat. "So what did Bradley have to say?" I reported the conversation and when I had finished, Holmes said, "Yes, those are the three I had thought of. I must admit I hadn't considered Harrods, but I think you are right in that regard. Suppose you go to Lewis while I visit Inderwicks, and we'll meet at Fribourg & Trayer. Then we can get some lunch because I am certain you will have worked up an appetite."

I agreed and Holmes then called for the page and asked him to secure two cabs for us. Holmes sent me off in the first cab, and some twenty minutes later, I was standing outside of Robert Lewis's cigar shop. I entered and was immediately overwhelmed by a sea of pleasant aromas. I spoke to a young man and asked if he carried German tobacco. He seemed confused by my question and referred me to an older man in the rear of the shop.

I introduced myself and repeated my question. "We used to carry several types of German cigarettes as well as Von Eichen tobacco, but there was so little demand for them, so we discontinued both perhaps five or six years ago."

The disappointment on my face must have been obvious, for he quickly added, "If you have your heart set on Von Eichen, I can special order some for you, but it will be quite dear." After assuring him it wouldn't be necessary, I left the store and decided to walk to Fribourg & Treyer. I headed down King Street, walked through St. James Square Park and emerged on Charles II Street. I then made a left on Haymarket and a few minutes later, I was inspecting the pipes in the window of Fribourg & Treyer. I could see I had arrived ahead of Holmes and contented myself in the pleasant weather.

Several minutes later, I saw him walking towards me, and while Holmes can usually mask his emotions, I was pretty certain, he had met the same fate at Inderwicks as I had at my assignment. "Third time's the charm," I said.

"Let's hope so," he replied tersely. We entered the shop and Holmes began to look around, examining the different types of cigars and tobaccos. I contented myself by examining the packets of rolled cigarettes. Finally, a middle-aged man approached Holmes and said, "May I help you, sir?"

"I certainly hope so," he replied. "In fact, you may be my last hope. I have a brother-in-law who is Austrian and will smoke nothing but tobacco grown in that region. Between you and me, I find his attitude rather snobbish; still, he is my sister's husband. He has a birthday coming up, and I thought I might buy him some of his favorite tobacco. Do you carry Von Eichen loose leaf?"

The man had smiled during most of Holmes's tale, but he stopped smiling and seemed a bit nonplussed at the end. "You are just out of luck, sir, but I believe I may be able to help you," he said. "How soon do you need the tobacco and how much would you want?"

"Since it seems rather difficult to come by, I should like to order a pound and perhaps you can suggest a good tobacco jar as well."

"I can certainly place that order and we will have it here within the week. As for storage containers, please step this way," and he proceeded to turn towards a shelf displaying jars and tins."

Holmes followed him and picked up a tather ornate Mason jar. As he examined it, he inquired nonchalantly, "What did you mean when you said, 'I was just out of luck?'"

The salesman looked around and then said in a conspiratorial whisper, "We had a gentleman in only this morning who purchased what remained of our Von Eichen – perhaps a quarter pound or so, and like yourself, he placed an order for more of the same – only he ordered two pounds."

"The gentleman you speak of," said Holmes, "was he perhaps 60, with dark hair going to grey at the temples, a full beard and a slight German accent?"

"No indeed, sir, I should say he was no more than 40, clean-shaven, with short blond hair and the bearing of an ex-soldier. If I may say, sir, he was quite a large man and he did have an accent of some sort."

"Well, thank goodness, it's not my brother-in-law." After examining various other containers, Holmes said, "Perhaps I'll choose one when I return. You said the tobacco would be here within the week?"

"Indeed, I'll add your order to the other gentleman's and both will go out tonight."

Holmes then paid for the tobacco and when we left the store, anyone could have seen the grin on his face. "Finally, Watson, a lead we can follow and which may actually direct us to our quarry."

"What will you do, Holmes?"

"I will assemble the Irregulars, and assign them in shifts of four to watch the store. We have no idea what day or what time Fritz will be in to pick up Edelman's tobacco; in the meantime, there is little we can do but wait."

Although Holmes could be as patient as Job – and here I thought of the many long vigils we had shared – when things were totally beyond his control, forbearance had never been one of his strong suits. I considered bringing this fact to his attention, but decided to refrain and let him enjoy the idea that we might finally be closing in on the elusive Edelman.

Upon our return to Baker Street, Holmes let it be known that he wished to meet with Wiggins, and less than fifteen minutes later I heard the leader of the Irregulars clambering up the stairs.

Before the lad could knock, Holmes bellowed across the room, "Do come in Wiggins."

The lad entered and said, "I 'eard you was lookin' for me, Mr. 'Olmes."

"Indeed, Wiggins, I have a most important commission for you and the lads." Holmes then described the hulking Fritz and the location of Fribourg & Treyer. "Sometime within the next week, that man will visit that shop. I need you to keep an eye on the premises at all times. In fact, I want you to stay on and watch an hour past closing each day. Also, make certain you are there before it opens. When the fellow shows up, I need you to follow him. The most important thing is to make certain you are not seen, so put your best boys on it."

"You can count on me, Mr. 'Olmes," Wiggins replied.

"I'm paying double the usual rate, and make certain each watcher has a pound in case he needs to take a cab." With that Holmes extracted several £1 notes from his pocketbook. "Here's the first week's wages and a quid for each watcher's cab fare, should it be needed."

Wiggins saluted smartly, grasped the money and headed for the door. As he reached it, Holmes said, "One more thing, Wiggins. I'll expect any cab fare that's not used to be returned."

Wiggins smiled impishly and said, "Righto, guv," and then he was gone.

Holmes then turned to me and said, "Well, that's one half of the problem that seems to be if not under control, at least manageable. Now, I must turn my attention to the other half of the problem, because should Fritz elude the Irregulars, we are going to have to be prepared for the worst."

"Other half of the problem? You can't be serious. I thought once we captured Edelman and Fritz, this would all be over."

"And it may well be," said Holmes, "but this has always been a decidedly two-part problem. I had hoped to avoid dealing with the second part by resolving the first in short order. However, as that is patently not the case, we must now focus, at least to some degree, on the other difficulty."

"What am I missing?" I asked.

"You know what I know, Watson. You have been with me nearly every step of the way, so you may trust me when I say Edelman is but a portion of the problem. It may well end with him, but on the off-chance that it doesn't, I want to be prepared."

"Blast it, Holmes, must you always be so opaque?"

"I'll try to steer you in the right direction, Watson. Consider the crops."

"Considering that this whole case has been about nothing but crops, that's really not much of a hint."

"Well then, if you find those words insufficient, I'd suggest you resort to the old French adage: *Cherchez la méthode*. With those parting words he threw himself into his chair and refused to say anything further.

I soon grew tired of hectoring Holmes, and focused my attention on the endangered wheat crop. However, no matter how I turned and twisted the problem, whatever had struck Holmes, certainly failed to strike me. I thought of the original French expression, *Cherchez la femme*. I then focused my thoughts on the women we had encountered, and it struck me that this whole affair had been brought to our door by the sister of a woman who had enjoyed a romantic liaision with the King of Bohemia. Was Holmes dropping a rather suggestive hint? Could Miss Serena Adler have been sent our way deliberately, and, if so, to what end?

The more I thought about it the more preposterous my theories became. Finally, I put those thoughts aside and began to consider what our next move might be. As I have often remarked, the man can be absolutely maddening at times.

Chapter Eleven

The rest of the evening and much of the next day were passed in silence as Holmes retrieved one commonplace book after another from his bookshelves. He read voraciously and smoked incessantly. Occasionally, he would pluck at his violin. Hoping for a better tomorrow, I turned in early and was surprised at how quickly I fell asleep.

When I awoke on that Monday morning, I expected to find Holmes in much the same position as I had left him, and I was not disappointed. "No developments, I trust?"

"It's early, Watson. The Irregulars are just taking up their positions, and I rather doubt the tobacco will arrive before the end of the week."

"How will you contain yourself, old man? At least, I have patients I can see, and they will occupy some of the time. Of course, I could take a few days off and keep you company."

"Thank you, but there's no need for that. I have a number of tasks to which I must attend." Having said that he disappeared into his room and reappeared some 30 minutes later in one of his favorite disguises, that of a weathered seaman who was quite obviously down on his luck.

"Pray tell, are you heading back to the docks?"

"Aye," he said, flashing his blackened teeth in a wide grin. "There are one or two shops down there that need visitin'," he offered, sounding more like a Liverpudlian than a Londoner. "I may be gone all day. I don't think I can hire a jobe with these clobber."

"What on Earth did you just say?"

He laughed and replied, "I don't think I can get a taxi or jobe in this clobber or these clothes."

Stunned by his preparation, not to mention his familiarity with the slang of Liverpool, all I could manage was, "Is there nothing I can do to help?"

"Send a message to Mycroft, and inquire whether Steven Roberts has returned from America, and if he has, see if Mycroft can arrange a meeting. And now, ta-ra."

I wondered whether to contact Mycroft at his office or the Diogenes Club. I soon decided discretion would be better served by sending a message to his club. I sat at my desk, and despite the fact that I am a writer, I willingly admit I struggled while composing that missive. Finally, when I thought I had the tone just right, I summoned the boy in buttons and directed him to deliver my letter to the club in Pall Mall. "There is no need to wait for a reply," I told him. Then I slipped a few coins into his palm and sent him on his way.

I spent the rest of the morning seeing patients at Barts and feeling guilty for having neglected my practice. By noon, I had made a small dent in the backlog and was weighing whether to soldier on and tackle some of the notes that needed to be written or enjoy a leisurely lunch and then return with a renewed vigour. Fortunately, my decision was made for me when an orderly knocked on my office door and said, "I have a message for you, Dr. Watson."

It was a letter from Mycroft. I opened it and saw that I had been summoned.

Lunch at DC at 1.

M

Obviously, the club had forwarded my message to his office. Looking at my watch, I realized I just had time to clean up and make my way to Pall Mall. I didn't want to be late, for I was well-aware of the role Mycroft played in Her Majesty's government.

Some twenty minutes later I descended from the cab and made my way into the Diogenes Club. Once again I was escorted to the Stranger's Room where I found Mycroft waiting for me.

"So good of you to join me, Doctor. I took the liberty of ordering lunch for you. I do hope you like roast chicken."

After I had assured him roast chicken was a staple of my diet, he asked, "Has Sherlock made any progress?"

Before I could answer, Mycroft rang a small bell, and a waiter, who had obviously been waiting close by in the hall opened the door, wheeled in a trolley and we sat down to eat. "Merlot, Doctor? It's an excellent vintage," stated Mycroft as he poured himself a generous glass. Although I usually refrain from drinking at lunch, I was well aware of the reputation of the cellars at the Diogenes Club, so I acquiesced and was very glad that I had.

"Do tell me what you and Sherlock have been up to," said Mycroft as he savoured a piece of the tender chicken.

I explained about the tobacco and our intention to have either Edelman or his henchman followed.

"Splendid! Splendid!" Mycroft exclaimed. "Anything else?"

I then explained how Holmes had said it was a two-part problem. "Ah," he sighed, "I was wondering when the penny would drop for my brother. Speaking of Sherlock, I assume he is out somewhere in one of his disguises – the docks, no doubt."

Despite everything I knew about Mycroft and his considerable skills, I was still dumbfounded by the fact that he had been able to divine his brother's destination, not to mention that he had gone there incognito. I then remembered to ask Mycroft about the mysterious – to me, at least – Steven Roberts.

At the mention of the name, Mycroft smiled. "It appears that I may actually have to exert myself to some small degree – what a repugnant thought – if I hope to remain one or two steps ahead of Sherlock. Please tell him that I have contacted Dr. Roberts, who has returned from abroad, and he is already pursuing several areas of inquiry as we speak." Then he looked at me with an expression I can only describe as owlish and said, "Wouldn't it be amusing if Sherlock encountered Roberts on the docks?" Then he chuckled and almost to himself muttered, "It's most unlikely, but …" and left the thought unfinished.

As we were almost done with lunch – Mycroft eats quite rapidly – I remembered to ask him about the question that was haunting me. "Have you made any progress with the anti-fungal?"

"We have made some progress, but as you might imagine, testing such a solution takes time. Unfortunately, plants grow slowly and we have to wait for them to mature to a certain point before we can ascertain the efficacy of our concoction. Fortunately, our adversaries also have to wait, so if I were a betting man, I would say we have at least another few weeks before they can begin to deploy the blight. Let us hope that is enough time to foil their plans – either by a solution from the laboratory or the actions of my brother and yourself."

I left the Diogenes feeling only slightly relieved. I knew we had some time, but not much, and of the two solutions suggested by Mycroft, I was inclined to trust my friend who had proven himself resourceful more times than I could remember and in a few situations that seemed every bit as perilous as this one.

I made several stops on my return to Baker Street, and when I entered the flat I was not surprised to discover Holmes had not returned. I sat at my desk and began updating my notes on this case – wondering if it would ever see the light of day or if Mycroft, as he had done on one or two previous occasions would "suggest" I withhold it from publication "for a period of time."

So engrossed was I in my work that I hardly noticed the passing of the hours. I was mildly surprised when I heard Holmes on the stairs. He entered the flat, and it was impossible to read his expression. I couldn't tell whether the day had been productive or an exercise in futility.

Some fifteen minutes later, he emerged from his bedroom. He had removed the makeup, brushed his teeth and slipped into his mouse-brown dressing gown.

"Whiskey?" I offered.

"Please," he replied.

I poured him a generous measure and then an equal amount for myself. "Shall you go first or I?"

"You, please,"

I then recounted my conversation with Mycroft, including all the pertinent details, and I even mentioned his brother's rather enigmatic remark about Holmes running into Dr. Roberts on the docks.

"Well if I am to see my old friend, it must happen on the morrow as today was singularly unproductive."

"Oh? How so?"

Before Holmes could answer, I heard the front door bell ring, followed a minute later by heavy footsteps on the stairs and then a knock on the door to which Holmes replied, "Do come in, Inspector Gregson."

With that Inspector Tobias Gregson entered the room. His was a familiar face as we had worked with him on a number of occasions. Today, he seemed anxious and perhaps a bit angry.

"I am so glad to find you in Mr. Holmes," said Gregson.

"What is on your mind, pray tell? And what is a Scotland Yard inspector doing on the docks at Wapping?"

Gregson started and began to ask, "How could you..." but then caught himself, "Very good, Mr. Holmes, but you'll have to explain to me how you deduced that."

"The soil on your shoes, Inspector. That very dark, grayish, brown silt loam is found in very few places in London, including the docks at Wapping, and when I detect the faintest aroma of sea air on your coat, what else can I conclude? Now, would you care for a whiskey?"

"Maybe a wee one," he replied. "I have to go back to the Yard and do the paperwork on this case, but a little bracer never hurt anyone, did it?"

After I had served Gregson and he had taken a sip, Holmes said, "So what brings you here this evening, Inspector?"

"There has been a murder, Mr. Holmes. A most unusual one, too, I might add."

"Do tell," replied Holmes, who was suddenly all ears.

"A sailmaker by the name of Elias Quince was found dead in his shop."

"Nothing unusual about robbery, Inspector," I replied.

"That's the thing, Dr. Watson; nothing of value was taken. There was some £20 in the till plus change, and Mr. Quince's wallet, which contained another £5, was found on his person."

"You said 'nothing of value' was taken. Was something taken, Inspector?

"It appears the order book has gone missing, but the dead man might have placed it anywhere. I'm certain it will turn up tomorrow when we search the place thoroughly."

"How was he killed, Gregson?" asked Holmes.

"That's the worrisome part, Mr. Holmes. It appears as though someone literally squeezed the life out of him. Without an autopsy, I can't tell if he suffocated or there were internal injuries that contributed to his death. The body is being taken to the coroner's as we speak."

"Besides the order book, were any goods taken?" asked Holmes.

"That too remains to be determined. I think we'll know a great deal more tomorrow when we go through the inventory with his sales clerk."

"Was the deceased a big man?" asked Holmes.

"He was of average height with a slender build. In all ways, he appeared a totally unremarkable individual."

"Where was the clerk when Quince was killed?"

"Quince had sent him home around 4 o'clock. He told the lad he'd close up. However, shortly before the young man reached his flat, he stopped in a shop. At that point, he realized in his haste to enjoy the extra hour of free time, he had left his pocketbook in his apron. When he returned and entered the shop, he found Quince dead behind the counter."

"My word," I exclaimed.

"Had business been slow?" asked Holmes, "Is that why the lad was sent home early?"

"No, according to the clerk, business had been quite good, and Quince had received a special commission which he had been staying late every night to work on, so the lad thought nothing of it."

"Obviously, Quince was meeting someone, and either he or the person he was meeting had insisted upon privacy."

"That's exactly what I was thinking, Mr. Holmes," said Gregson. "Great minds…" and he left the rest of the sentence unfinished.

It took all my self-control not to chuckle, and I was afraid to look at Holmes so I kept my eyes averted.

"And you'd like me to take a look?" asked Holmes.

"If you would be so kind," replied Gregson.

"Well, I'm quite busy on another case right now, but perhaps I can spare you a few hours tomorrow morning. What time are you meeting the clerk and where is the shop located?"

After Gregson had provided the name and address – Elias Quince, 42 Wapping High Road – Holmes promised to meet him there at nine the next morning.

When the inspector had departed, Holmes looked at me. Normally, he is inscrutable, but I could sense that he was agitated. "What's wrong, Holmes?"

"This could have been prevented, Watson, if I had only moved a bit sooner."

"How could you have saved a man you didn't know?"

"What do you think I was doing all day? I was visiting sailmakers; unfortunately, for Mr. Quince, I started upriver where the docks are shallower and there are more sailing vessels. Had I started downriver, I might have encountered him today and quite possibly saved his life."

"But why were you visiting sailmakers in the first place? And why was this man killed?"

"If I am correct, he was killed because they are tying up loose ends. You heard Gregson say business was good, and nothing was taken. And the way he was killed…"

"Yes, Gregson said it appeared as though he'd been crushed to death."

"Have we encountered anyone in this case who might be able to perform such a feat?"

"I haven't, no."

"But I have."

"Fritz!" I exclaimed.

"Exactly," replied Holmes, "and Quince's death also erases any threads that might tie the deceased to Herr Edelman."

"Oh Holmes, this grows more monstrous by the day."

Then as if he had had enough conversation, Holmes suddenly became quiet. He took out his violin, but he didn't play. Rather, he sat morosely before the hearth, picking aimlessly at the strings. Anyone who didn't know him might have thought he was daydreaming. However, I had seen him adopt that pose in the past, and I knew that he was deep in thought. I also knew he would be no fit companion for the rest of the evening.

He didn't touch the supper Mrs. Hudson brought up, and when she came to clear away the dishes, I explained that he was in a brown study and trying to solve a most important case.

"I've known Mr. Holmes long enough that no explanation is necessary, Doctor," she said. And then she whispered, "I just hope he has his appetite back by breakfast."

The next morning, I was up at half seven. Holmes and I ate in silence and then we hailed a cab and instructed the driver to take us to 42 High Wapping Road. I sat in silence watching the great city come to life as we made our way towards the Thames. The roads were crowded, and it took us nearly an hour before we arrived at our destination.

Quince's shop was a modest affair from the front. A sign hanging above the door proclaimed in bold red letters against a blue background, "Elias Quince, Master Sailmaker, Custom Sails Made to Order." Above the lettering was a three-masted clipper whose sails were billowing in the wind. Gregson was standing in front of the shop with a young man, who I presumed was the clerk. When the inspector made the introductions, I learned that the young man's name was Roger Walker.

As he shook our hands, he said, "I've read all about you, Mr. Holmes."

To which Holmes replied, "Don't believe everything you read."

We then entered the shop, and Walker showed us where he had found the body behind the counter. "So anyone passing on the street would think the store was empty," Holmes said.

"I suppose so, sir," replied the lad.

Holmes bent down and examined the floor. "No signs of blood." Looking up at the lad, he asked, "How tall was Mr. Quince?"

"Perhaps five foot seven inches," replied the clerk.

"So he could have been easily overcome by a much larger man?" suggested my friend.

"I rather doubt that, sir. Mr. Quince was quite strong for his size."

"Given the fact that everything seems to be in order and nothing has been knocked over, I think we can safely assume Quince knew his assailant."

"That seems reasonable," said Gregson.

"And the only thing missing is the order book?" asked Holmes.

"Yes, sir," replied the lad, "as far as I can tell."

"Did Mr. Quince seem out of sorts lately? Had he been acting differently in any way?"

"He was quite jovial these past few weeks. He even gave me a bonus last week of an extra five quid."

"Do you have any idea why he did that?"

"As well as being a sailmaker, Mr. Quince had come to fancy himself something of a scientist lately. He was always looking for ways to improve the quality of his sails. Last week, I think he made some sort of breakthrough. He was in a generous mood all week. A few of the customers even remarked to me about his sudden change in demeanour."

"Do tell?" said Holmes. "When did this preoccupation with science start? And can you tell me about any of the procedures with which he had experimented?"

"I suppose it started about three or four months ago. I know that he began by experimenting with applying different types of paints and varnishes to canvas and lately he had moved on to other materials."

"When you say 'other materials' can you be a bit more specific?" asked Holmes.

"I wish I could, sir. But Mr. Quince had become quite secretive over the past few weeks, and that's when he started sending me home early."

"Do you think he was trying to hide something from you?"

"Maybe, sir. All I can tell you is that he was a fair boss but a demanding one. When he gave me time off, I wasn't about to argue with him."

I chuckled to myself at the lad's honesty.

"Where did Quince do his work and where did he keep his supplies?" asked Holmes.

"There's a workroom in the back. Quite often, he would be in there tinkering or repairing a sail and I would attend to the customers. If it was a particularly large order, I would often find Mr. Quince in one of the sheds out back. In one he kept bolts of canvas and other types of cloth. For large or special orders he would often retire to the larger of the sheds which he had recently renovated into a second workshop or laboratory. Like I said, lately he had begun to think of himself as a scientist."

We made our way into the workroom. It was neat and orderly with various tools hanging from pegs in the walls. There was a workbench with two bolts of canvas leaning against it. Holmes examined everything minutely with his lens. I heard him grunting and occasionally talking to himself, but after about twenty minutes he seemed satisfied and asked to be shown the sheds.

When we entered the yard, we saw two small buildings although one was slightly larger than the other. Holmes went to the smaller one first, but it was locked. "If you would just look the other way for a moment, Gregson." No sooner had the inspector turned his back than Holmes went to work on the lock with his picks. In less than a minute he had it open.

When Gregson turned around, Holmes handed him the lock and said, "My mistake, Inspector. When I examined it closely, I discovered it wasn't really locked at all."

Gregson smiled and said, "Just let me know beforehand when you're going to 'examine' the other one, Mr. Holmes."

Holmes pulled open the door, and we saw more bolts of canvas on rough wooden shelves and an assortment of buckets and trays on the floor. "Interesting," said my friend, "but more or less what one might expect to find at a sailmaker's shop."

We then made our way to the second shed, the larger of the two. Gregson obligingly turned away once more, and Holmes had the lock picked and door open in no time. In addition to wooden shelves filled with bolts of cloth, this building contained a large workbench fitted with a vise, an assortment of tools and hanging on the door was an old slicker that appeared to be missing an arm.

Where the smaller shed had no windows, this second one had two windows on the rear wall. Holmes examined both carefully. "These look new," he remarked. "I wonder…" and he let the sentence trail off.

Holmes began by examining the bolts of cloth. "Curious," I heard him say to himself. When he had finished, I inspected the cloth. There were various types of canvas, including cotton, flax and one that I thought might have been hemp. I was also surprised to see a bolt of what I believed was silk mixed in among them.

Gregson stood in the doorway watching us carefully while we prowled about the shed. As Holmes knelt by the workbench, examining some pails and shallow trays that were coated with a white mixture, he suddenly looked up and said, "Watson, would you see if there is a lantern in the other shed, and Gregson, I would much appreciate it if you would ask Mr. Walker to join us. I have a few more questions."

As Gregson headed toward the rear entrance of the shop, I returned to the first shed. Fortunately, Holmes had not secured the lock so I was able to let myself in. As there were no windows, I opened the door wide and began to examine the shelves on both sides for a lantern. After a few minutes, I returned to Holmes who was already questioning Walker.

"These windows are relatively new," I believe. "Would you know when they were installed?"

"Perhaps two months ago, sir. As I said Mr. Quince had recently had it renovated. After working out here for a week or so, he was complaining the shed was too hot, so he hired a carpenter friend of his who put them in."

"You've been here how long, Mr. Walker?"

"I'm starting my sixth year."

"Had Mr. Quince ever complained about the heat before?" asked Holmes.

"Not that I can recall," replied the lad.

"And he worked here often?"

"Lately, he was out here just about every day, sir. As I said, I tended to the counter while he made or mended sails."

"Thank you, Mr. Walker. I appreciate your cooperation. If you should find the order book, you will let Inspector Gregson know?"

"I certainly will," the boy said.

Then Gregson added, "I'm going to give the store a thorough examination, as well as both sheds. After that, I'll head to Mr. Quince's home in Lambeth. If I find anything, including the book, Mr. Holmes, you'll be the first to know."

"Thank you, Inspector. I appreciate your assistance as well."

As we left the shop and were walking along Wapping High Street, I said to Holmes, "That didn't seem like a terribly productive morning."

"On the contrary, Watson, I believe we learned a great deal."

"Oh, would you care to enlighten me?"

Holmes smiled and then said, "I should like to call your attention to the new windows."

"I thought they might prove significant."

"Indeed."

When I looked as puzzled as ever, Holmes said, "There are any number of reasons one might install windows. I trust you can put the chain together."

With that he hailed a passing cab, and upon entering, he leaned back against the cushion, closed his eyes, sunk his chin to his chest and said nothing for the entire ride back to Baker Street.

Chapter Twelve

For the rest of the day and all of the next, Holmes remained sullen and morose. As the Irregulars filed their reports every few hours about the activity at Fribourg & Treyer – none of which included any sighting of either Fritz or Edelman – Holmes became more and more disagreeable.

I was glad I had a full day at the hospital the next day, and for a few hours I escaped the tension which seemed to have enveloped us since we had learned of the potential implications of this case.

When I arrived home that evening, Mrs. Hudson greeted me before I could ascend the stairs. "I must say, Dr. Watson, I'm more than a bit worried about Mr. Holmes."

"I know he's not been himself these past few days, but ..."

"I understand you're working on a case of some importance, and I've learned to take it in stride when he is short with me, but he's not eating at all, and the parlour is so fouled with tobacco smoke."

"I'll speak with him, Mrs. Hudson. You have my word."

"Thank you, Doctor."

I was fully prepared to take Holmes in hand, but when I entered the flat, I found him sitting his chair, staring into the hearth with his fingers steepled under his chin. It was a pose with which I was all too familiar. He was deep in thought – no doubt turning over the myriad difficulties posed by the case in search of a solution.

I decided to postpone any sort of confrontation until he seemed a bit more amenable. An hour later, Mrs. Hudson served our dinner. On the way out, she looked at me and I mouthed the words, "Not yet." She nodded and left the room quietly.

I sat at my place, and asked, "Holmes, won't you join me?"

He looked at me and I said gently, "I know this case is consuming you, but you must be at your best if you are to bring it to a successful conclusion."

At that, he smiled wanly and said, "That seems less and less likely with each passing hour – let alone each passing day."

"What on Earth do you mean?"

"We know our man; we know his plan – so it's really just a matter of waiting. I believe you said as much yourself," and then he lapsed back into silence.

A few minutes later, he looked at me and posed what I considered a most unusual question, "Doctor, do you think you could lose yourself in the city of London? Could you find a burrow and remain out of sight for an extended period of time until you absolutely needed to emerge?"

"As long as I had access to food and water – and of course tobacco, I'm certain I could manage such a feat."

"Excellent! I am certain you could as well. Consider, at present, London encompasses approximately 122 square miles and has a population of some 4 million people. You just admitted that you could conceal yourself for a prolonged period if you had provisions. By contrast, England encompasses an area of more than 50,000 square miles –

much of it rural and isolated – with a population of around 30 million souls. If we add Scotland and Wales, that's another 38,000 square miles. I trust you begin to see the scope of the problem."

"Yes, but you have a lead – the tobacco."

"Exactly, my friend, we have *a* lead – one. If that should fail, I am not quite certain what our next steps might be, nor do I feel like considering the catastrophic consequences. No, Watson, this case hangs by the thinnest of threads, and that slim line, which appears to be under considerable stress, offers no guarantees."

Having said his piece, Holmes joined me at the table and proceeded to pick at his dinner. Although he tried to maintain an air of camaraderie, I knew the problem and the threats it posed frightened him even as it consumed him. I made a mental note that I would remain close by his side until there was a break in the case. I rationalized my decision by telling myself that such a course of action would allow me to watch him, make certain he ate – and that I would be ready to help at the spur of a moment.

After dinner, Holmes once again busied himself with his commonplace books while I attempted to read. The few conversations we did have seemed laboured, so rather than force the issue, I decided to turn in early.

When I awoke the next morning, I immediately summoned the boy in buttons and sent him to Barts with a note explaining that I would not be available for the foreseeable future. "You know you really don't have to remain with me, Watson. I'll be fine."

Once again, I was taken aback when I realized he had divined my thoughts, but then I considered the change in my routine and the fact that I had written the note before eating, and I saw the chain of events just as he had. "I am sure you will be fine, but I've come this far, and I'd hate to miss out on the conclusion."

"I don't think you need concern yourself with that. I'm certain we have not even approached the final act. Still, your consideration is appreciated." We ate in silence, and Holmes was in a state of perpetual motion after breakfast. He couldn't sit still, nor could he focus. Finally, about half nine, he said, "I think I'll go check on the Irregulars – in disguise of course. Although I must say a few of them have become quite good at spotting me despite my best efforts at camouflage."

I had to laugh because I don't think I had ever penetrated one of his disguises. "What will you be today? Banker? Costermonger? Captain of industry?"

"No, I was thinking more of a Roman Catholic priest. I don't believe the lads are familiar with that one. I haven't used it in some time."

With that Holmes turned to go to his bedroom. He stopped abruptly when the front bell rang several times in rapid succession. "What on Earth?" I exclaimed.

That was followed by the sounds of young legs running up the stairs as fast as possible and a sudden pounding on our door. "Mr. 'Olmes! Mr. 'Olmes!"

I opened the door to find one of the Irregulars – a lad named Nicky – bent over trying to catch his breath. "What's wrong, my boy?"

"Is Mr. 'Olmes 'ere, Doctor? It's important that I ..." At that point, Holmes joined me at the door. "Oh, Mr. 'Olmes. We spotted 'im – that Fritz fella."

"Calm down, Nicky, and begin at the beginning," Holmes cautioned the boy.

"Wiggins and me had the first shift. We got to the shop about 15 minutes before it opened. There was a cab parked right in front of the door, but we just figured 'e was waiting for a fare. No sooner does the key turn in the lock then the bloke, Fritz, jumps from the cab and rushes inside.

"Wiggins goes over and he's pettin' the horses, but 'e really wants to hear where the driver's goin'.

"So, the bloke comes out after a few minutes carrying some packages, and Wiggins 'ears 'im say 'St. Pancras Station.' So we hires a cab and follows him. He goes into the station, and we're a minute or two behind. The bloke buys a first-class ticket for a train leaving in two minutes. So I gives Wiggins all my money so he can buy a ticket, and then he tells me to come 'ere and tell you everything. I had to run all the way, but Wiggins says he'll report when 'e can."

"My word, Holmes, but these are some resourceful lads you've recruited."

"That they are, but I shall never forgive myself if anything should happen to Wiggins." Holmes turned back to Nicky, "Did you happen to learn where the train was headed?"

The lad smiled. "Of course, sir, I knows better than to give an incomplete report. The last stop was Dover."

I had to smile in spite of myself. At that, Holmes said to me, "Would you ask Mrs. Hudson to prepare a hearty breakfast for Nicky. I should think that's the least we can do." He looked at the lad, "You are hungry, aren't you?"

"I'm always 'ungry, Mr. 'Olmes. And though I've only tasted it once or twice, I'm quite taken wif Mrs. 'Udson's cooking."

I wasn't certain how our landlady would react to such flattery, but she took my request in stride. When I returned back upstairs, I asked, "Do you think they are possibly fleeing the country?"

"I shouldn't think so. I rather suspect Fritz will disembark at one of the stops between here and Dover, either Ashford or Canterbury, but I suspect that a quick escape to the Continent figures into their plans at some point."

"Well, we've certainly eliminated a great many of those 50,000 square miles you were fretting about, and our one lead appears to be holding solid."

"Indeed, now we are back to waiting. Let's just hope that Wiggins is as resourceful as I think he is."

That morning seemed to drag on forever. Both of us tried to busy ourselves, but Holmes proved more successful than I as he studied an array of maps that included all the areas on the way to Dover as well as those portions of the country on the coastline north and south of the port.

Around half two in the afternoon, the bell rang and a few minutes later, Mrs. Hudson knocked on the door. "Telegram for you, Mr. Holmes."

Holmes bolted to the door and practically snatched the telegram from our landlady's hand. Then he caught himself, "I apologize Mrs. Hudson, it's just that this is a matter of some urgency, so I thank you for your promptness," and then he looked at me, and I nodded, "and for your patience as well."

I could see that Holmes's words, while they may have caused him a bit of consternation, had greatly mollified our long-suffering landlady. As Holmes turned away from her, she smiled at me before departing.

No sooner had the door closed than he had torn open the envelope and read it aloud.

In Canterbury. Will wait here for you.

W

"I knew Wiggins would come through!" I exclaimed.

"I never doubted it," echoed Holmes. "Now pack a bag for an overnight stay and then grab your hat – and your pistol – for we are off to Canterbury."

A few minutes later we were in a hansom on our way to St. Pancras. We arrived at the station just as Big Ben was sounding the hour in the distance, and by the time we had made our way to the ticket window for the South Eastern Railway and purchased our tickets, we learned that we had just missed the 3:05 train and the next one wasn't scheduled to depart until half four.

While we waited, Holmes sent a number of wires. But it wasn't until we were on the train that my suspicion was confirmed. "I'm assuming one of those telegrams was to your brother, apprising him of the latest developments and of your intention to head to Canterbury."

"Yes. I think at this point, Mycroft needs to know our every move and our plans so he can prepare a backup plan should one become necessary."

Although I understood Edelman was a dangerous man, Holmes's blunt words – not to mention the implied suggestion of failure – suddenly put everything, including my own mortality, into perspective for me. Unconsciously, I patted my coat pocket and was somewhat reassured by presence of my revolver.

When we arrived in Canterbury some two hours later, I was surprised to see that Wiggins was not waiting on the platform for our arrival. I wondered where he might have got off to. After waiting a few minutes, we decided to find a place to eat since the center of town was but a short walk. We soon happened upon a rather pleasant looking public house, The Three Mariners, which I subsequently learned had the distinction of being the oldest such establishment in town.

After arranging for rooms – Holmes registered under the name Hudson while I used my own name, it being far more common than his – we entered the dining room, which was empty except for a man and a boy sitting all the way in the rear. I was stunned when the youngster suddenly jumped up and waved to us. It was then that I realized the boy was Wiggins although I had no idea who his companion might be. By now, Wiggins had reached us and he said, "Mr. 'Olmes, I thought you'd never get 'ere." As he uttered those words, the man he was eating with stood up and turned to face us. Words failed me as I found myself staring at my cousin Henry's tenant – Nicholas Tagliamonti.

"What on Earth?" I blustered. "How? What are you doing here?" I asked of Tagliamonti. "And why are you having supper with Wiggins?"

Holmes, who had been taking in the scene, turned to me and said, "Let's join them so that we can conduct our business with a modicum of privacy." Although Holmes is generally loath to discuss anything of importance in public, the fact that we were the only ones in the pub seemed to have allayed his fears.

When we were all seated, Holmes looked at Wiggins and asked, "What of Fritz?"

"I followed him 'ere," replied the lad, "but there was a carriage waitin' for 'im, and I didn't 'ave any money for a cab, and I knew I'd need money to send the telegraph. So I followed 'im on foot as far as I dared, and then I came back 'ere, wired you and met this gentleman in the telegraph office."

Turning to Tagliamonti, Holmes said, "What shall we call you? Nicholas? Tagliamonti? Or would you prefer Capitano?"

At that Tagliamonti burst out laughing while I must admit to being totally in the dark. Finally Tagliamonti spoke, "Well done, Mr. Holmes? What gave me away? And by the way I am only a lowly *tenente* – a lieutenant in your language – but feel free to call me whatever you like."

"As you wish, Lieutenant. As to what gave you away, I have written a small monograph on tattoos and am quite familiar with the symbol of the carabinieri." Pointing to Tagliamonti's hand, Holmes added, "I should imagine you keep that covered when you are working incognito in Italy."

"I certainly do, but I saw no harm in leaving it uncovered here, plus it fit right in at the docks."

"As I suspected," remarked Holmes. "Now to the more important question: *Why* are you here?"

"We had a number of small farms lose their wheat crop in the areas surrounding the Po Valley last year. Our investigation revealed that all the farms had been leased by the same German gentleman, a Mr. Robert Edelman.

"Working with the Surete, we discovered several more farms with failing wheat crops in western France. And we also became aware of the fact that Mr. Edelman had made his way to England."

"But how did you end up at my cousin's house? Was it just a coincidence or is there something more sinister at play here?"

"I assure you, Dr. Watson, there is nothing untoward taking place. I was sent to England and told to find a room in Manchester. I was astounded to learn that Henry was a cousin of the famous Dr. Watson and even more taken aback when I discovered that you and Mr. Holmes would be visiting. When you left, I breathed a sigh of relief as I thought I had passed muster – but obviously in the final analysis, I would have been found wanting."

"But why Manchester?" I pressed him.

"Two reasons, through one of our informants – all of whom had been alerted to the situation – we had heard about the failing farm outside the city, and also because I was tracking certain supplies Edelman had ordered. He paid a great deal of extra money to have those products shipped via Manchester rather than having them arrive in London and proceed from there."

"Would you care to enlighten us as to exactly what Edelman was shipping?"

"I have no problems telling you, Doctor, but I think it would be best if I cleared it with my superiors first."

Although I was disappointed, as a former military man, I could certainly appreciate his respect for the chain of command.

Holmes then interrupted my train of thought when he asked, "And I suppose you followed the goods from Manchester to here."

"In Manchester, I helped unload the ship myself, Mr. Holmes. Once I knew where they were bound, I simply headed directly here and have been biding my time waiting for them to arrive on the train." Turning to me, he said, "I told your cousin it was a family emergency. I would greatly appreciate it if you would be kind enough to explain everything to him when the opportunity presents itself, Dr. Watson."

I assured him that I would and then I asked, "And how, pray tell, did you wind up sharing a meal with Wiggins here?" I asked.

"I've been watching every train. When I saw Edelman's right-hand man, Fritz, leave for London yesterday, I was certain he'd be returning with the goods, but such was not the case. However, I was intrigued by this lad here, who was quite obviously following Fritz – he's quite good at it, you know. At any rate, when he returned to town I followed him and watched him enter the telegraph office. I then wandered in and managed to overhear him sending his communique to you. Since I was pretty certain he was stuck here without funds, I introduced myself, and we have spent the afternoon waiting for you to arrive. We would have met you at the station, but we appear to have lost track of time."

"I was sure you'd be on the train before the last one," Wiggins said.

"We missed it by minutes," I explained.

"At that point, I offered to buy the lad dinner, and then you arrived perhaps forty-five minutes later."

"So if Edelman is still waiting for supplies, they must be in transit." Turning to Tagliamonti, Holmes inquired, "Do you have any idea where Edelman is staying?"

"Yes, I made a few discreet inquiries and bought a few rounds of ale at a public house. Edelman has leased an estate called Red Fox Lodge. It's located perhaps five miles outside of town and as you might expect, it is quite isolated."

I knew well what Holmes thought about the country, and once again he seemed to have been proven right. Whatever deviltry was being concocted at Red Fox Lodge, it would not have been detected by the law until it was too late.

"Tomorrow, I want you to reconnoiter Red Fox Lodge. Edelman knows Watson and myself, so I am afraid the task falls to you, Lieutenant. Perhaps you can devise some ruse that allows you to enter the home. As a trained operative, I'm sure I don't have to tell you what to look for."

"And what will you be doing, Mr. Holmes?" asked Tagliamonti.

"Dr. Watson and I will be making a pilgrimage to Ashford. By the way, how many crates were unloaded from the ship for Mr. Edelman?"

"All told, there were four. Three were marked fragile and the remaining one was significantly heavier than the others. It was impossible for one man to lift."

"Thank you, Lieutenant."

Wiggins who had been listening intently suddenly piped up, "What do you want me to do, Mr. 'Olmes?"

"I want you on the first train to London in the morning. I will have letters for you to deliver to Inspectors Lestrade and Gregson as well as my brother at the Diogenes Club."

"Can I 'ave breakfast before I go?" he asked.

"Of course, my lad. As soon as you arrive in London, go to the Diogenes Club. If my brother is not there, proceed to his office in Pall Mall. I'll give you the address. After that, head directly to Scotland Yard. Watson and I will see you off in the morning; in fact, we'll travel with you as far as Ashford as I want to get there as soon as possible."

And so it was that at half six the next morning, Holmes and Wiggins and I were enjoying a breakfast of sausages, eggs, toast and tea. Wiggins devoured his food with relish and I found the fare filling if nothing else. As for Holmes, he picked at his food, but he did drink three cups of coffee.

Shortly after seven the train pulled into the station and Holmes and I climbed aboard for the relatively short ride to Ashford where we bid Wiggins farewell.

"Now, what do we do?" I asked.

"What we've had to do so often in the course of this case: We wait. But first, I need to rent a wagon and procure a few tools. I don't know what else we may need beyond that just yet."

"You're hoping to intercept the crates being delivered to Edelman?"

"You are scintillating this morning, Watson. Yes. We have forty minutes before the next train for Dover pulls in. Although I understand money is no object to our friend, I'm curious as to why he paid to have things purposely shipped via a longer route? My guess is he was being extra careful in case we had tumbled to his plan in London. Although it doesn't appear to make sense, but if we have learned one thing about Edelman, he is eminently practical and quite cautious."

"You make it sound so easy, but it appears that we have a long day in front of us."

"That may be true, old man. Fortunately, we have to consider only those trains coming through with a baggage car."

For all his cleverness, sometimes Holmes misses the mark completely. Every train that came through that day had a baggage car, and while Holmes easily gained access to the cars, telling the porters that he was Edelman and he had changed his mind and now wanted the crates delivered to his workshop in Ashford instead of his estate in Canterbury, it was a long morning as each inspection proved fruitless.

Finally, a train arrived shortly after three, and in the baggage car were four crates on which had been stenciled in all upper case letters – ROBERT EDELMAN, RED FOX LODGE, CANTERBURY. They had also been numbered 1 OF 4, 2 OF 4, etc. While Holmes was arranging to have the crates placed in a wagon, the porter pointed to one and, "That one's quite heavy. It'll take two men at least to move it."

After we had unloaded the first three – all of which had also been marked FRAGILE – Holmes turned his attention to the last. Although he could push it across the car, he could not lift it by himself. Between the three of us, we managed it although I think Holmes did most of the heavy lifting. I have often remarked on how my friend's appearance belies his rather prodigious strength. Still, I will readily admit none of this was accomplished without a great deal of sweating and a few mild oaths.

After we had covered our cargo with a blanket, we drove a few miles outside of town, and turned down an overgrown lane. "I don't think this is much used," said Holmes who then climbed into the back with a pry bar he had

157

extracted from a satchel. "While I am working here, go to the mouth of the lane and keep an eye out for any passersby, Watson. I shouldn't like to be caught doing this."

From my position about fifty yards away, I watched as Holmes got the first top off. After some digging through what I thought was wood wool I saw Holmes remove a large glass container – perhaps five gallons but certainly no less than three – which appeared to be filled with water. I watched as my friend carefully prised off the top and put his nose to the opening.

"Can you tell what it is?" I asked.

"There is no discernible aroma," he remarked.

"Have you any idea what it might be?" I asked.

"I have my suspicions," he replied.

I then watched as he carefully replaced the stopper, closed the container and placed it back in the crate. He then repeated the process with a second box and eased off another lid. He reached in and I couldn't tell exactly what he was doing, but a few minutes later he had resealed the crates, using a hammer from the satchel. Then he summoned me back to the wagon.

"Here's what we must do. I need you to take the next train to Canterbury and tell Tagliamonti the crates will arrive tomorrow morning. Also find out whether Edelman has someone waiting at the station as we did here, or if he has made arrangements to have someone notify him when the crates arrive, or has he made arrangements to have the crates delivered to his home. That last part is extremely important. Most important, make certain you are not seen by Edelman if he should be in town. Check the platform before leaving the train."

"And what will you be doing?"

"I have a few chemical tests I need to run. I'm going to drive you back to town and put you on the train. Then I'm going to send a telegram to Mycroft, visit an apothecary's shop and remain out of sight with these crates. Tomorrow morning, I would like you to catch the first train back here, and if everything falls into place, we will load the crates back onto an incoming train from London and make certain they are delivered to Canterbury."

"So you've devised a plan?"

"Let us call it a work in progress. There is still a great deal to be done and several disparate elements need to fall into place before I can ever begin to consider it a plan."

"Still, I believe we have done more with less in the past."

"Good old Watson, you remain the one fixed point in an ever-changing universe."

Holmes waited with me on the platform, perhaps fifteen minutes, for the next train. I could see he was anxious to be off, but despite my urgings, he remained by my side. As the train pulled out of the station, he gave me a quick wave, and the last image I had of Holmes that day was of him climbing aboard the wagon. I knew he was headed to an apothecary although the why of it eluded me.

I vowed that I would press him for an answer as soon as time permitted. At that moment it struck me that we had no idea of how much – or how little –time we had left.

Chapter Thirteen

Upon returning to Canterbury, I asked after Tagliamonti, but he was nowhere to be found. Finally, around half six, I went down to the taproom for supper. I had just ordered when Tagliamonti wandered in. Before I could call to him, he spotted me. No sooner had he sat down than he said in a low voice, "Where is Mr. Holmes?"

I recounted our day in Ashford and then asked about the crates that were to be delivered on the morrow. "Do you know if he has made any type of arrangements for them?"

Tagliamonti smiled at me, and said, "I thought Mr. Holmes might want to know that. I've made inquiries at the station, and from what I understand, they are to notify Edelman the moment the boxes arrive. My guess is Fritz will be despatched to collect them."

I concurred with his estimation. Although I must admit, in the back of my mind, I wondered how Holmes would feel about his "guess."

"Were you able to visit Red Fox Lodge?"

"I hired a dog cart and drove past it. It's quite a large piece of property. The lodge, a handsome three-storey red-brick building, is set well back from the road, perhaps a hundred yards or more. Behind the lodge there is a veritable forest of old-growth trees. I wouldn't be surprised if some of the oaks and yews were several centuries old. It seems to me an ideal location for a fox hunt."

"Do you have any idea of the size of the estate? I feel certain Holmes will want to know that."

"Then I have anticipated both you and Mr. Holmes. I visited the local solicitor, who arranged the rental for Edelman. According to his records, the estate encompasses some several thousand acres. It measures approximately three miles from end to end along the road and extends back from the road some four miles. However the back end of the estate broadens to a distance of almost five miles."

"That is an enormous piece of property. I assume there are a number of outbuildings."

"You assume correctly, Doctor. There is a large barn, an even larger stable, and several other structures that may be workhouses or storage sheds. There are also kennels for the hounds although they are no longer used. The servants all sleep in the lodge, except for the gamekeeper and the stablemaster, both of whom have small cottages behind the stable."

"Well, you are a wealth of information."

At that point, my food was delivered and after we had both ordered pints, I said to Tagliamonti, "Aren't you hungry?"

"I've already eaten," he replied.

"You'd be surprised what you can learn by listening to the locals after standing some of the lads to a round or two in the pub."

"But there's been no one in this pub."

"Apparently, most people prefer the food and the ale at The Parrot. Truth be told, so do I," he laughed.

We chatted about an array of things as I ate, and then Tagliamonti surprised me when he said, "I wonder how much longer it will be before they try to put their plan into motion."

"I'm sure Holmes will have a much better idea of that than I. Why don't you ask him in the morning?"

"I'll make a point of it," replied Tagliamonti.

The next morning I boarded the 6:05 from Canterbury to Ashford. I had told Tagliamonti we would not be back until sometime in the afternoon, but that we would meet him for supper in the taproom of The Three Mariners. A short time later, I disembarked from the train and found Holmes waiting on the platform for me. He was standing next to a man in his mid-forties. He was a very distinguished looking individual, with glasses and a full head of hair cropped short that had mostly gone grey.

Holmes made the introductions, "Watson, I'd like you to meet Dr. Steven Roberts. He is one of England's foremost chemists."

We exchanged pleasantries, and then Holmes must have seen the enquiring look on my face. "After I telegraphed Mycroft, he arranged a special train for Dr. Roberts, and we spent most of the night discussing how best to deal with the chemicals which Mr. Edelman has ordered.

"I cannot be certain, but I believe Edelman is quite close to putting his plans into action, so we needed to move with a great deal of alacrity."

"It's important, Mr. Holmes, that this Edelman fellow be made aware of his options."

"You have my word, Dr. Roberts."

"In that case, I think you have developed a brilliant strategy. Considering the stakes, would you like me to remain in case I can be of further assistance?"

"That would be splendid, Dr. Roberts. I appreciate the offer and intend to take full advantage of it."

When the next train pulled in about thirty minutes later, Holmes approached the porter and said in a very posh Kentish accent, "These crates were mistakenly delivered to me yesterday. I believe they are intended for my brother in Canterbury." He then slipped the porter a note and said, "Mum's the word, eh? I wouldn't want anyone to get into a pickle. My brother can be a proper gumption when it suits him."

The porter thanked Holmes profusely and promised the boxes would be delivered without a word being said to anyone.

After we had left the station, Dr. Roberts looked at Holmes and said, "That was amazing, from the pronunciation to the local patois. I grew up in Maidstone and I know a Kentish man when I hear one. Tell me, Mr. Holmes, in what part of Kent were you born and where were you raised?"

I had to laugh and said, "Doctor, don't be fooled. Holmes is no more from Kent than I am; it's just that he is an inordinately talented actor – with a special gift for mimicry."

I'm not certain Roberts believed my explanation, but he looked at Holmes with a new-found appreciation for his abilities. At any rate, we retired to the closest public house and enjoyed a hearty Kentish breakfast of bacon, sausages, potato rosti and eggs.

Holmes said little and I could see he was considering the myriad possibilities that might come into play if his plan were to succeed.

Dr. Roberts and I talked about medicine, and he explained that after years of tending to the sick, he had decided to devote himself to research in an effort to eradicate the causes of disease and misery. "The great thing about researching infectious diseases is the bacteria don't talk back."

I had to laugh at the notion of a man peering through a microscope and getting into a heated debate with a staphylococcus.

I was mulling that over when he asked me why we hadn't taken the train to Canterbury with the crates. "There is always the possibility that the man picking up the crates, who is familiar with Holmes and perhaps myself, though I cannot say for certain, might see us and thus we would lose the element of surprise."

Suddenly Holmes broke in, "Quite right, Watson. They have no idea how close to them we are; therefore they labour, as Chaucer might have said, 'in blissful ignorance.' We must keep the element of surprise on our side until just the right moment."

Later that day, we boarded the train to Canterbury. Along the way, Holmes described both Fritz and Edelman to Dr. Roberts, "Watson and I will remain on the train until you have made certain they are not in the vicinity. If you see anyone resembling either of those descriptions, come back to the platform and wipe your forehead with your handkerchief. If you do, we'll just continue on to Dover and return on the next train. Be waiting on the platform when it arrives and if it's safe to disembark, please remove your hat; otherwise, we will spend the night in Ashford and return on the morrow."

We sat on the far side of the car when we pulled in and Roberts was the first one to disembark. A few minutes later he appeared at the other end of the platform wiping his forehead. "That might have been a narrow escape," said Holmes as the train pulled out and we continued on to Dover.

When we pulled into the port city, we had twenty minutes before the train was scheduled to begin its return run. We found a small tea shoppe and ordered coffee. The place was fairly busy with people who were arriving for the boat to Calais and others disembarking from the steam packet that had tied up a few moments earlier.

After we had finished, we returned to the station and purchased two third-class tickets for Ashford on the off-chance that we would be unable to leave the train at Canterbury. As we pulled into the station, I could see Roberts standing on the platform, craning his neck and looking about, as though he were waiting for someone. However, before I could say anything, Holmes remarked, "His hat is still on his head, and he doesn't seem inclined to remove it. It looks as though we'll be spending another night in Ashford."

It was hard to gauge Holmes's mood as we rattled along, but finally he remarked, "I wonder why they were in town for such an extended period of time. I should have thought Edelman and Fritz were getting close to setting their plan in motion."

"Perhaps they've had a setback of some sort," I ventured, "or maybe they are waiting for something else to be delivered."

"I'm certain you are correct, Watson. At any rate, we won't know anything until tomorrow at the earliest."

Back in Ashford, we took rooms at The Wailing Siren and were just about to have lunch when the proprietor of the inn entered and said, "I have a telegram for you, Mr. Hudson." I had almost forgot Holmes's *nom de guerre*, but I caught myself in time. Holmes took the envelope, thanked the publican and slipped him a few coins.

As he read it, I wondered who might have sent it. As though he were reading my thoughts, he said, "It's from Dr. Roberts. What do you make of it?"

Second shipment arrived. Workers quite busy.

SR

"Interesting, is it not, Watson?"

"Obviously, your caution paid off. Other than that I'm at sea."

"Workers, old man. Up until now, we knew about Edelman and Fritz, and I had always allowed for the possibility of one or two other subordinates. The phrase 'Workers quite busy' suggests that I may have underestimated their numbers."

"What's to be done? Do you want to involve Lestrade and Gregson?"

"I go back to the point that up until now, Edelman and Fritz would appear to have broken no laws. However, what we need is a distraction of some type. That will allow us to deal with those two blackguards on our terms, and once you have cut the head off the snake…"

"The snake dies," said I, finishing his thought for him.

"I'll be right back, old man. I just need to send a quick wire and hope for the best."

Holmes was gone for approximately ten minutes during which time our lunch arrived. Although I had had a proper breakfast, I was enjoying a cold beef sandwich with pickles when Holmes reappeared. "I have asked for a reply," he said as he sat down and began to eat.

"From whom?"

"Watson, you should know my methods by now. If we cannot turn to the official police…"

"Holmes, you can't involve the Irregulars. This is much too dangerous."

"I quite agree, old man, so let's see if you can figure out what our next move is."

Since I was uncertain of exactly what type of distraction he had in mind, I had no idea to whom we could turn for assistance. Although I was tempted to admit my shortcomings, I could see that Holmes was enjoying my predicament. It may seem petty, but I had decided two could play at that game, so I told him, "Let me mull it over and consider the possibilities."

"Excellent, and while you're doing that, I'm going to enjoy my pipe."

We finished our lunch in relative silence, and I could see that the forced inactivity was chafing at my friend. I am certain that had he brought his makeup, he would have disguised himself and caught the next train to Canterbury. However, Holmes had anticipated a brief stay as had I, we had not packed a great deal. Still, I had learned from experience to bring along my sidearm just in case.

After we had left The Wailing Siren, Holmes made a few inquiries and learned that the closest library of any significance was in Maidstone, the largest town in Kent, some twenty miles away. "If I were going to make the journey to Maidstone, I might as well return to London and conduct my research in a proper library," he groused.

"I wonder if any of the local solicitors might be of assistance," he mused.

"If they needed a solicitor, why not just select one in Canterbury?"

"Because said barrister would be in ready reach of anyone making inquiries in Canterbury. No, if I were Edelman, I'd seek legal advice from someone at least one town removed and quite possibly two."

"What exactly are you hoping to learn?"

"I'd like to know as much as I can about Red Fox Lodge and the lands surrounding it. That is where our foes are ensconced and that is where we will confront them. The more we know about the place and its environs, the better we can plan."

Having said that, he entered the post office we were passing and returned a few minutes later all smiles.

"What have you discovered?"

"There are but four solicitors in Ashford."

"Is there anything I can do to help?"

"Indeed. I'll take two and you take two, and we'll compare notes when we've finished." He then gave me the names of and addresses of the offices. "What am I to tell them?"

"Tell them you are a retired military man who has done well in the market and is now hoping to retire here. Make it known that you are looking for a large estate – preferably one where you could ride to the hounds. I'll meet you for supper at half six in the taproom."

I am never comfortable prevaricating, but I did my best as I spoke to Sidney Edwards of Edwards & Parker and then Robert Shaw, a transplanted Irishman, who had moved to Ashford forty years previously. Neither man could suggest any properties near Ashford although Shaw informed me that a large estate named Red Fox Lodge had come on the market the previous year, but had been leased almost immediately.

As he described the property, I pressed him for details. When he had finished, I told him it sounded perfect for my needs and while he offered to make some inquiries I said that wasn't necessary, and I would continue looking elsewhere. "If you find anything in Kent, and you should require my services, please feel free to contact me." I assured him that I would and then headed back to the hotel.

I looked in the dining room and didn't see Holmes, so I headed up to my room intending to take a short nap before dinner. My head had just hit the pillow – or so I thought – when I heard a gentle rapping at my door.

I opened it to find Holmes, and he was smiling. "How long have you been asleep?" he asked.

"Just a moment or two," I assured him.

"Really? You know it's almost seven, and we were supposed to meet at half six."

I looked at my watch and was stunned to see that nearly three hours had passed. "My apologies, Holmes, but it has been a rather long day."

"No apology necessary. Did your visits to the solicitors yield anything we might use?"

"I don't believe so." I then informed him Edwards had been no help whatsoever while Shaw had described the property to me in some detail."

"Oh, what did he say?"

"He told me there is a large wine cellar, that the bridle paths are extensive, and fox hunts used to be a regular part of the season there when Lord and Lady Foley owned the house. After Lord Foley passed, his wife, who detested the cruelty involved in the activity, ceased it altogether."

He looked to be getting bored, but he asked, "Anything else?"

"Apparently there is a formal garden and a tennis court along with an archery range which could also serve as a shooting range and to round things out there are two or three large ponds which are stocked with fish on a regular basis. Finally, there is quite a sizable lake where visitors can go rowing or sailing, depending upon their preference."

"My word," exclaimed Holmes, "a man might never have to leave the grounds."

"Oh, and one more thing, one of the outbuildings can be set up to serve as a makeshift chapel."

After I had finished, there was something in his eyes – a gleam if you will – and I could tell some detail in my description had caught his attention. Although I was tempted to ask him, I decided to indulge his flair for the dramatic, knowing he would reveal all when the time was right.

"And you? How did things go with your visits?"

"Not nearly so well as yours, I'm afraid. One of the solicitors just moved here about a year ago, and the other was of even less help, if you can believe it."

"So you have no good news to share?"

"Actually, that's not quite true. I received word that our reinforcements will arrive tomorrow morning. I've arranged a meeting for noon here so that I can bring everyone up to speed."

The thought that we might soon be joined by others made me smile for I had come to appreciate what a formidable foe Edelman was, and – truth be told – I was looking forward to bringing both him and his henchman, Fritz, to justice. After all, one of them, presumably Fritz, had murdered Elias Quince, the sailmaker. An action, no doubt carried out at the behest of Edelman.

The next morning I went down for breakfast to find Holmes sitting with Tagliamonti and enjoying tea. "I trust you are fully recovered from yesterday's exertions. We waited to order until you came down."

"I'm sorry to have delayed your breakfast."

"No need to worry, Doctor," said Tagliamonti. Just then a young woman appeared and Holmes and I ordered bacon and eggs while Tagliamonti opted for sausage. After the food had arrived, Tagliamonti asked, "So what's the plan, Mr. Holmes?"

"I'd rather not repeat myself, so let's wait until we are all assembled either today or tomorrow. Then I will outline everyone's roles and answer any questions that might arise."

Although Tagliamonti seemed a tad miffed, he acquiesced. Holmes, seeming to sense it, tried to put him at ease saying, "I can tell you this much. I want you to precede us to Canterbury. I will wire a friend, Dr. Steven Roberts, and he will meet you on the platform. We will follow behind on the first afternoon train. If Edelman or Fritz is in the vicinity,

I want Roberts to stand on the platform. If the coast is clear, both of you will be waiting for us when we arrive. Understood?"

"I understand, Mr. Holmes, but do you really think such elaborate precautions are necessary?"

"Consider the stakes, Lieutenant. The European economy is at risk. I don't think we can be too careful."

Chastened a bit, Tagliamonti said, "My apologies, Mr. Holmes."

Holmes merely nodded and said, "I can appreciate your exuberance, but we must temper that enthusiasm with an abundance of caution."

We finished our breakfast, and Holmes looked at his watch and said, "I think we should make our way to the station." En route, he stopped at the telegraph office and sent a wire to Roberts. I must admit to feeling a bit of relief as we waited for the train to arrive. At long last, we were preparing to meet our adversary with a coterie of men capable of subduing such a fiend.

My step may have even been a bit more jaunty on the way to the station, so you can imagine my dismay when the only person to get off the train was a woman. I thought our reinforcements must be arriving on the next train. However, when she turned to face us, I heard Holmes say, "It's so nice to see you again, Miss Adler," and there standing in front of us was Irene Adler's sister – Serena – all by herself.

Chapter Fourteen

Holmes performed some quick introductions between Miss Adler and Tagliamonti even as he was urging the Italian to board the train. Before I could say anything, Holmes reminded our new friend, "If all goes well, we will be on the 1:20, hopefully looking for both you and Dr. Roberts on the platform."

No one said anything until after the train had departed, and then Miss Adler turned to Holmes and said, "Your wire made it sound as though the situation were quite serious. And can you really hope to capture the man responsible for my sister's and Godfrey's deaths?"

To say I was confused would be an understatement of epic proportions. Then I reflected upon all the times I had put my faith in Holmes, and he had yet to disappoint me. Even though I was bursting with questions, I held my tongue, knowing Holmes would explain all when it suited him.

"I believe I can," replied Holmes. "However, it won't be easy, for he is as clever as he is ruthless."

"Just tell me what to do, Mr. Holmes."

"This afternoon we will travel to Canterbury, and if all goes well, we will join forces with two men, one of whom you just met. When we are all together, I will outline my plan and tell each person what is expected of him or her. In the meantime, would you care for a cup of tea?"

Perhaps because I was so anxious to get Holmes alone and pepper him with questions, the morning dragged on inexorably. It was interesting listening to Miss Adler talk about herself and her escapades with her sister. I fancied Holmes paid particular attention to the latter tales.

Shortly after one o'clock, we boarded the train for Canterbury and when we pulled into the station, I saw Roberts standing on the platform by himself. We were just getting ready to depart for Dover when Tagliamonti ran onto the platform and joined him. Holmes was quicker than I and he jumped up and informed the porter that we had changed our minds and decided to disembark here.

"Don't lose your tickets; otherwise, you'll have to purchase new ones to get you to Dover," the porter advised us.

Holmes assured him that we would be very careful and then he thanked him. A minute later, the five of us were gathered on the platform.

When we had alighted, Holmes looked at Tagliamonti who said, "Fritz was just here, and I wanted to make absolutely certain he had left town before I joined Dr. Roberts on the platform."

"And has he?" asked Holmes.

"He picked up a few things at the greengrocers and then he stopped at the ironmongers. He came out with something in a sack. I followed him to the edge of town and then ran all way the back here. It appears as though I made it just in time."

After he had imparted that bit of information, introductions were made between Miss Adler and Dr. Roberts, and then Holmes suggested we retire to The Three Mariners. After rooms were secured, Holmes asked the proprietor if there were any sort of private dining room that we could use that evening.

"I have a storage room that I can put a table in for you. It's clean and tidy, but it won't hold but more than ten."

"Well, since there are only five of us that should be splendid. We should like to dine at seven."

"I'll have the room ready, sir," he said with a smile as Holmes slipped him a couple of notes.

"Things appear to be falling together rather nicely, Watson," he said.

"Let's hope they continue to do so."

"I'm sure you have an abundance of questions, if you can hold them until our meeting after dinner, I would be most appreciative."

A few hours later the five of us were treated to a truly delightful dinner that included fresh asparagus and turnips from the owner's garden, roasted lamb, and concluded with a freshly baked apple crumble and coffee. When everyone had had their fill, Holmes cleared his throat. "What I am about to tell you must remain secret. The future of England, perhaps the Continent, may well depend upon your discretion, bravery and love of country."

Holmes then recapped everything we had experienced thus far – with a few careful omissions. He concluded by saying, "As you can see, we are facing an incredibly dangerous and resourceful man. If he is allowed to disseminate the spores he has cultivated, it's impossible to say what the repercussions might be.

"And the most frustrating aspect of this is the fact that up until now he has broken no laws that we can prove. England has never faced a threat quite like this, so as you can imagine, there is no legal way to forestall his actions, let alone incarcerate him for them. The potential for economic damage and possible loss of life due to this nefarious plot is virtually incalculable."

Holmes then proceeded to outline his plan in general terms. "Tomorrow, the three of you will hire a Clarence and take it to Red Fox Lodge. I have already taken the liberty of sending a wire to Edelman, using your name Lieutenant but obviously without your title, informing him you are quite interested in leasing his property for a few months in the autumn and winter and possibly purchasing all or a portion of the estate if you find it to your liking."

"But he doesn't own it," Tagliamonti said.

"Quite so," replied Holmes, "but I've yet to meet a criminal who will walk away from ready money, and you'll be offering a great deal of it. Also, he has incurred considerable expenses thus far, so he may see this as a form of reimbursement for his troubles."

"Dr. Roberts, you will act as the estate agent, while Mr. Tagliamonti and Miss Adler will pose as a married couple, Mr. and Mrs. Birch, interested in the property."

"And what will you be doing while we are bearding the lion in his den?" asked Miss Adler.

"Dr. Watson and I will be attempting to put an end to his scheme once and for all. Have no fear, we will be on the estate, and if we are successful, we will come to the main house and attempt to bring both Edelman and Fritz to justice. Now, I must warn both Miss Adler and Dr. Roberts there is a great deal of risk involved. So I will understand if you bow out in which case I'll have to make other arrangements; however, that would certainly give Edelman more time to put his plan into action and escape."

"Before you go any further, Mr. Holmes, you can count on me," said Miss Adler with a certain degree of ferocity in her voice.

I cannot say for certain whether Tagliamonti or Roberts or both were swayed by the young woman's determination, but they immediately pledged their loyalty to our little conspiracy.

At that point Tagliamonti left the room and returned with a bottle of claret and five glasses. "It's not Italian wine," he said looking at the label with a certain degree of disdain. "Still, I'm told that France can produce the occasional vintage that is palatable."

We all laughed and after he had finished pouring everyone a glass, he said only, "To success."

We all shouted, "Hear, hear," and I believe that simple gesture bound us all together a bit more tightly.

After he had tasted his wine, Tagliamonti looked at my friend and said, "Now, Mr. Holmes, as you were saying."

Holmes then produced a map from his pocket and unfolded it. "This is a map of the property surrounding Red Fox Lodge. Here is the road in front – the route you will be taking. Dr. Watson and I will be entering the grounds by another track altogether," he said pointing to a point on the map. "It is essential that you arrive at exactly one o'clock and if possible that you occupy Edelman and Fritz for at least an hour – and it is equally imperative that you keep them both in the lodge. Insist on a tour of the house if possible, but should he also suggest a tour of the grounds, make some excuse – such as a pressing engagement elsewhere which would preclude a full excursion – and see if he will commit to another date."

We talked late into the night, defining and redefining each person's role. As you might expect, Holmes tried to take into account as many contingencies as he possibly could. When we finally emerged from our cloister, the only person in the taproom was the publican who was sitting on a stool with his head on the bar fast asleep.

After the others had left, Holmes gently roused him, settled the bill and added a generous gratuity. The next morning, both Holmes and I slept in as we didn't want to possibly encounter the others on the street. After all, Holmes had reasoned, "You never know who is watching."

I had coffee and toast and then retired to my room where I tried to occupy my mind re-reading Wilkie Collins's *The Lady in White.* I had read it several years earlier, and I must admit the plot reminded me of some of the more – to use one of his favorite terms – *outré* adventures Holmes and I had shared throughout our long association. Around noon I knocked on Holmes's door, but there was no answer, and I had no idea where he might have got to. When I had returned to my room and was putting the key in the lock, I saw him ascending the stairs. He was wearing a false beard and muttonchops.

"Just give me a moment to remove these, will you, old fellow?" he said as I followed him into his room.

"What were you up to?"

"I was merely observing from a distance in an effort to see if anyone happened to be following our comrades; so far the coast is clear."

"Do you really think Edelman is aware of our presence here?"

"I do not know, but I'd prefer not to take any chances in that regard. Now it's nearly noon, what say you to a very quick lunch and then we must set out."

After a bowl of soup and a lager, Holmes and I hired a dog cart to take us some ways out on the road that led to Red Fox Lodge. After perhaps twenty minutes, Holmes stopped the driver, whose name we had learned was Miller. Pointing to the land on the right, he asked, "Do you know whose property this is?"

"Aye, sir," replied the driver, "that be the Todd family estate – Lord Christopher and Lady Susan."

Pointing down the road towards Red Fox Lodge, Holmes inquired, "And who owns the next parcel?"

"That belonged to Lord Lanigan, but he's passed and his wife has leased it to some foreigner. She's now living in London, I believe."

"They don't shoot trespassers, do they? My friend and I were of a mind to do some bird-watching," Holmes said, holding up a pair of field glasses.

"The Todds won't mind at all, so long as you're not hunting. Can't speak for the foreigner though; he keeps to himself pretty much."

"Well, we are armed only with binoculars, a compass, and our notebooks, so we must hope for the best."

"Would you like me to come back later?" the driver asked. "It's a long walk back to town."

"That would be splendid, but as we are on unfamiliar terrain, we might lose our way, and you'd have come all the way out here for nothing."

"Suit yerself," said the driver.

Holmes then paid the man, and he quickly turned his horse around and headed back to town. He then turned to me and asked, "We are armed with something more than field glasses and a compass, I hope?"

I tapped my coat pocket and answered, "Indeed, we are."

We then set off into the field in front of the woods at a 90-degree angle from the road. After we had walked for thirty minutes, Holmes said, "I believe if we turn left and walk for approximately another twenty-five minutes, we should find ourselves quite close to the large lake on the grounds of Red Fox Lodge. From there we will make our way under cover of the woods towards the lodge itself."

With the sun high in the sky, the day was quite warm and while there was a pleasant breeze, I was glad when we finally reached the cover of the woods. After walking some distance, I spotted the lake in front of us through the trees. We drank from a stream and then Holmes consulted his map. "We have perhaps three-quarters of a mile until we reach the end of the target range."

"Let us hope that no one is out hunting pheasant for dinner. I'd hate to come this close and get shot in a shooting accident."

"Really, Watson. They wouldn't be hunting pheasant until at least October, and the season for game birds doesn't begin for another two weeks."

"Ever heard of poachers, Holmes?"

He shushed me, and we continued in silence for another ten minutes or so, and then we came upon one of the strangest things I have ever seen. On the ground I could see logs that had been cut and then lashed together to form a sort of bridge or platform. However, there was no water, and the entire structure was covered with what I thought might be bales of hay which in turn were concealed by a heavy grey tarpaulin. The whole structure stood perhaps eight feet high, and it must have measured thirty feet from end to end.

Initially, I had no idea what to make of it, but then Holmes said, "Someone has erected a wall of some sort in an effort to forestall those hunting accidents about which you were so concerned."

The canopy of the trees came to the top of the wall, so for the moment we had no view of anything else. Holmes once again consulted his map and said, "If this is still accurate, there should be a large shed on the other side of the wall on the left, perhaps 150 feet away. It has an awning and should provide some degree of cover as we make our way to the lodge."

"I assume you mean by walking behind it."

"Of course."

All I could hope for was that the groundskeepers had been attentive to both the range and its environs.

By this time Holmes had walked to the very end of the wall and lowering himself to the ground, he discreetly peeked around it. He snapped his head back behind the wall and looked at me. "They are further along than I thought. I pray that we are in time."

"What makes you say that, old man?"

He gestured towards the end of the wall and said, "See for yourself."

I imitated Holmes and lowered myself to the ground, took a quick glimpse around the wall, and was stunned at the sight that greeted me.

I knew what I had seen, but for the life of me, I couldn't figure out what such a thing was doing in the middle of a field in Kent. After taking another quick look, I turned to Holmes and said, "What are they going to do with that?"

"Put their plan into action," he replied tersely. "I shouldn't be surprised if they have two or three others hidden away in different parts of the country."

"But if they do, they must have cost a fortune."

"Edelman is backed by the wealth of the German Empire, and the stakes he is playing for are incalculable. In this instance, Watson, what certainly seems like a great expense will pale in comparison to the returns it is anticipated to generate."

"Did you expect to find this?"

"In a sense I did, but I also didn't expect to find it guarded. You did see that man with the rifle?"

"He was rather hard to miss. So what's our next move?"

"Let me think for a bit," he replied, and after several moments of deep concentration, he said, "I have an idea. I just hope you are game for it, old friend." And then he told me exactly what he wanted me to do.

I must admit I was filled with misgivings, but as we were so close and their plan was so dastardly I decided the only thing I could do was soldier on.

"I'll do my best, Holmes," I said.

"That is all anyone can ask, old friend."

I put my field glasses to my eyes and slowly walked around the corner of the wall all the while gazing up into the trees. The guard, who was dressed in overalls and seemed more like a hired bumpkin than a trained professional, spotted me immediately and yelled, "Hey you! What are you doing there? You're trespassing and need to leave now."

"I say, I've just spotted an extremely raw hawfinch and am trying to trace it back to its nest."

"I don't care what you've seen. You can't be here."

"You don't understand," I said as I moved slightly along the wall, always keeping my field glasses trained upon the canopy provided by the trees above me." By now the man was fewer than ten feet away. "Would you like to see it? It may be the only one you ever see in your life."

I knew I had piqued the man's curiosity, and no sooner had he handed me his shotgun and put the glasses to his eyes then Holmes crept up behind us, took the shotgun from me and said, "Don't make a move."

We then took him behind the wall and trussed him up using his belt and braces. We also gagged him and as we stepped around the wall, I finally said to Holmes, "What exactly is that thing?"

Chapter Fifteen

Holmes smiled at me and said, "That is a dirigible."

I knew that it was a balloon of some sort, but it was significantly longer and far less round than the balloons with which I was familiar. Truth be told, it resembled nothing so much as a long, fat cigar. Hanging from it was an oblong gondola that appeared to be made of wicker. In the center of the gondola, I could discern what I thought was a heavy black kettle and attached to the framework was an engine of some sort, for I could see a propeller.

Looking at Holmes, I said, "You expected to find this here, didn't you?"

"Quite frankly, I was expecting to find a balloon of some sort. I must admit that the thought of a dirigible never crossed my mind."

"What is it for?"

"That is how they plan to disseminate the blight spores. A man walking through a field could cover only so much ground and infect only so many plants. And if a farmer ever saw him, well, who knows what might happen. However, men flying high above the fields and dropping spores, which are virtually invisible to the naked eye as they pass, could do a great deal more damage in much less time."

"And you said, you thought there might be more of these."

"I shouldn't be surprised if they had similar dirigibles hidden away in all the major farming areas – Norfolk,

Suffolk,Yorkshire, the East Midlands and Devon – and possibly even Cornwall."

"But why begin here in Kent?"

"Come, Watson, everyone knows the southeast section of the country, Kent in particular, is regarded as 'The Garden of England.' What better place to begin?"

"We had best destroy that ball-, dirigible as soon as possible. There's no telling what mischief Edelman and Fritz might get up to if they should ever get it airborne."

"Before we do that," Holmes began, "we need to ..."

Suddenly a booming voice ordered us, "Stand where you are Mr. Holmes." I looked in the direction of Red Fox Lodge and saw Edelman walking towards the dirigible. Fritz was some ten feet behind him, carrying a rifle, which was aimed at us. Walking between them with her hands bound and struggling mightily against being pulled by a rope held by Edelman was Serena Adler.

She started to speak, "I'm so sorry…"

However, she lapsed into silence when Edelman threatened her, saying, "Do be still, madam, or I shall have Fritz gag you."

Seizing the initiative, Holmes said, "What we have here is a standoff of sorts. I have a shotgun, Dr. Watson has a pistol, Fritz has a rifle, and you have a dirigible filled with hydrogen in which you would like to escape. Admittedly, you have a hostage which does tilt the scales slightly in your favour."

"Only slightly," laughed Edelman, "such chivalry."

"Don't worry about me, Mr. Holmes. Just shoot the balloon and then kill this monster," Miss Adler yelled.

Edelman went to strike her, but before he could, Holmes interrupted him saying in a steely voice, "That's not necessary."

Edelman turned back to look at Holmes with a surprised expression on his face. "I had almost forgot your quaint notion of gallantry."

Then he composed himself, looked at Holmes and chuckled. "I feel I should inform you, Mr. Holmes, that Fritz is far more than just a man with a rifle, as you put it. As you might have suspected, he is a former military man and an expert marksman. In fact, on a number of occasions, he has served as Master of the Hunt for the Kaiser. On one of those hunts, Fritz bested a certain Colonel Sebastian Moran in a special shooting contest, posting a perfect score from two hundred yards. Apparently, it wasn't even a close contest, except for the fact that Fritz allowed Moran to save face.

"So while you do have some cards to play, I believe ultimately you will lose all the tricks to my trump," he said gesturing towards Fritz.

"So then how do you propose we end this?" asked Holmes.

"It's quite simple: Fritz and I, along with your friend here, will fly away. We will deposit her safe and sound in some out-of-the-way village, and then I suppose the chase will begin all over again."

"I'm not certain I can agree to those terms," said Holmes.

"I'm not certain you have any other options," said Edelman, mocking my friend.

"You could release the woman, and I give you my word as a gentleman that we will not fire upon your dirigible."

"Your word as a gentleman," replied Edelman with a degree of sarcasm. "A gentleman doesn't break into homes. I am a gentleman, Mr. Holmes."

"Oh? I didn't think gentlemen bullied women nor threatened them. Perhaps it's only German gentlemen that do that."

I could see that Edelman was stung and searching for a retort. Finally, he said, "I wasn't aware that you are a – what's the term you English use – a blue blood."

"Nobility and honour are more than matters of heritage," Holmes replied rather tartly.

"No, I suppose you may be correct in that regard," answered Edelman, "although I'm not certain I totally agree. Still, I'm afraid you are going to have to do better than that if you want me to release the woman."

"Suppose I were to exchange the shotgun for the woman? Certainly that would greatly diminish any chance we might have to shoot down the dirigible."

"But Dr. Watson still has his pistol," countered Edelman.

"Dr. Watson is a man of medicine bound by the Hippocratic oath and the principle of *primum non nocere* – first, do no harm. Do you really think a man who has devoted his life to healing others would violate the sacred oath that has guided him throughout his career?"

Although I was seething at Holmes for using the basis of my profession against me, I couldn't argue with his reasoning.

"Also," Holmes asked, "The gondola doesn't look all that big, and she appears to be quite angry with you. Accidents do happen. Accept it. She's a liability and one who would definitely slow you down – or worse."

Holmes's words appeared to give Edelman pause. "I must admit, you make a most compelling case, Mr. Holmes." After another moment of reflection, he said, "Here are the terms: Dr. Watson is to remove his pistol and place it on the far side of the field," he said gesturing to his left. "After he has done that and rejoined you on your side of the field, I will release the woman."

"Agreed," said Holmes.

"And I have your word that neither you nor Dr. Watson will try to run across the field, take up the pistol and attempt to bring the dirigible down?"

"You do," said Holmes.

And then almost as an afterthought, Edelman smiled and said, "Nor will you allow the woman to do the same?" When Holmes again agreed, Edelman said, "Excellent, because they wouldn't get very far."

"You have my word," replied Holmes. Turning to me, he said, "Go, Watson, and leave your pistol on the far side of the field."

I trudged across the field. With each step resentment was growing in me. I removed my pistol from my pocket, placed it on the ground and turned to rejoin my friend. When I was about halfway back, I saw the large German open a gate in the gondola and quickly clamber inside. For just a second or two, I caught a glimpse of sacks piled inside to the basket. As I walked back towards Holmes, Fritz held up his rifle and kept it trained it on me.

Edelman said, "I can't tell how many game birds Fritz has brought down in his life, and Dr. Watson presents a far larger target than a grouse, so do give a care before you think of breaking your word or doing anything else foolish."

"You know it's not too late to end all this," replied Holmes. "We could say nothing, and you and Fritz could return home to Germany. It would be as though nothing had ever happened."

"I'm afraid that's impossible, Mr. Holmes," said Edelman as he climbed into the gondola, joining Fritz. "I was given a mission; failure is not an option."

Holmes then removed the shells from the shotgun and as Edelman untied the last of the tethers holding the dirigible down, Holmes handed the gun to Edelman barrel first and Edelman released the rope that had kept Miss Adler in check.

She quickly ran to my side and as the dirigible slowly rose into the sky, my focus remained on Fritz, who was still aiming the rifle at the three of us.

"Holmes, the gondola is filled with sacks. Do you think those are the spores?"

"I'm certain of it," my friend replied. Then he glanced at the ascending dirigible which appeared to be rising more quickly than it had initially, and cupping his hands to his mouth like a megaphone, he bellowed, "Do give a care. Air travel is fraught with peril. You can still quit."

"It's a risk I'm willing to take," yelled back Edelman as the dirigible continued to soar higher into the sky.

A sense of failure overwhelmed me. I couldn't imagine what Holmes must be feeling, so I turned to Miss Adler and asked, "They didn't hurt you, did they, my dear?"

"Nothing is injured except my dignity – being dragged about by a rope as though I were some sort of prize farm animal."

"How did they come to see through your charade?" I asked.

"As we sat down to tea, Edelman glanced at Tagliamonti and asked about the tattoo on his hand. When Tagliamonti said it was part of his family's crest. Edelman laughed and said, 'That's odd, it looks exactly like the symbol of Italy's carabinieri.'

"He continued to chuckle and said, 'I was warned about you, Senor Tagliamonti, just as I was warned about Francois Bencolin of the Surete and Sherlock Holmes here in England.' At that point, Fritz entered the room and while Edelman held a gun on us, Fritz tied up both Tagliamonti and Roberts and locked them somewhere in the cellar."

"I suppose we should go free them at once," I said.

"Oh they can wait another few minutes," remarked Holmes as he kept his eyes on the dirigible which was growing smaller and smaller as it rose into the sky and sailed towards the west.

"Why don't you retrieve your pistol, old friend, and then we'll go and see to our captured comrades."

I retraced my steps across the field, walking much more deliberately than I had just a few moments previously. I retrieved the gun, and as I looked up at the sky, I realized they were out of range for my pistol, and we were probably safe from Fritz's rifle.

As I trudged back towards Holmes and Miss Adler, my friend was shading his eyes and still staring up into the sky, an impassive look on his face. I couldn't imagine what Holmes must be thinking. Suffering a defeat was bad enough but to have been outwitted by a man whose evil intentions posed such a grave threat to the Empire must have been particularly galling.

I was perhaps twenty feet from them when I heard what sounded like a distant gunshot. For a second I thought Fritz might have fired on us despite Edelman's promise. I first looked at Holmes and saw that he hadn't moved but that his features were marked by a grim grin. Then I glanced up into the sky just in time to see the dirigible explode into a giant ball of flame.

In less the ten seconds the entire dirigible, gondola and all, had been enveloped in flames and just disappeared from the sky.

Holmes looked at me, over the head of Miss Adler, nodded almost imperceptibly and said, "Now, Watson, I think we should locate our friends and free them from wherever Edelman has imprisoned them. We can send someone back for Edelman's watchman later."

Without another word, he turned and started to make his way to the lodge while Miss Adler and I were left to wonder what had just happened.

Chapter Sixteen

We went back to the lodge and freed Tagliamonti and Roberts from the cellar. After I had explained everything that had transpired to them, Tagliamonti began apologising profusely for having been found out because of his tattoo. Roberts was relieved to be released, and all three were wondering what might have caused the dirigible to explode.

Although I had my suspicions, I decided to hold my tongue until we were alone. As it turned out I had to wait some time to get *all* my questions answered.

After we had gathered our belongings at the hotel, we went to the station and after a twenty-minute wait, the train pulled in. During that time, I heard several people remark upon the mysterious explosion in the sky earlier in the afternoon.

On the train, all five of us shared a first-class compartment – although I'm certain Holmes would have preferred different seating arrangements.

Normally laconic when traveling, Holmes found himself answering an unending volley of questions from three of his traveling companions. As you might expect, many of their queries focused on what might have happened to Edelman's dirigible. During the journey, Holmes displayed a rather surprising knowledge – if anything about Holmes can ever said to be surprising – about the history and evolution of manned balloon flights.

He began with the Montgolfier brothers, who developed the first hot air balloon, and demonstrated its potential for flight by sending animals into the sky in small baskets. Then he moved to Jean-François Pilâtre de Rozier and Marquis

François-Laurent d'Arlandes, who in 1783, made the first free, manned hot air balloon flight in Paris. After twenty minutes aloft, they landed miles away from the center of the city whence they had ascended. "Incidentally," Holmes added, "their balloon had been designed by the Montgolfier brothers."

"And from there the idea just took off," interjected Roberts, prompting groans from all around.

Holmes caught my eye before continuing, "That same year Jacques Charles and the Robert brothers launched the first manned hydrogen balloon flight from the Jardin des Tuileries in Paris." I wasn't certain why, but I committed that fact to memory.

"But they were all balloons, weren't they?" asked Roberts. "Where did the dirigible come from?"

"The dirigible is relatively new having been invented less than two decades ago in 1884. Two men, Charles Renard and Arthur C. Krebs, both of whom were serving in the French Army Corps of Engineers, devised an elongated balloon, which they christened *La France*. It turned out to be a significant improvement over earlier models. In fact, theirs was the first airship that could return to its starting point in a light wind. I trust you saw the rather crude engine attached to the gondola of Edelman's dirigible," Holmes said to Miss Adler.

"I wondered what that was," she replied.

"By the way," Holmes remarked, "I must commend you on your bravery and your willingness to sacrifice yourself."

"I'd have given anything to make him pay for Irene's death. I'm just glad that no one on our side was injured in the process."

I suppose that remark had a sobering effect on all of us, for we soon lapsed into silence – each of us content to be alone with his or her thoughts after such a harrowing experience.

When the train pulled into St. Pancras perhaps an hour later, we all promised to keep in touch. Everyone, with the exception of Holmes, was keen on the idea of dining together the next evening before Tagliamonti returned to Italy. I told them we could make no promises, but if our schedules permitted, we would join them at Rules at half seven. While we were chatting, Holmes excused himself and went to send a wire.

"What is so important that you can't share a meal with the people who helped us foil a serious threat to the stability of the Empire?" I asked once we were in the cab on our way to Baker Street.

"And besides, I have a number of questions I'd like you to answer, but I forbore asking them in front of the others."

At that Holmes smiled at me. It was a warm smile, uncharacteristic of my friend. "I owe you far more than answers, my friend. As I have remarked upon more than one occasion, you have the grand gift of silence. I beg you to indulge me for just a few more hours and then I promise to answer all of your questions and hold nothing back."

Of course, I acquiesced. We had just entered our flat, when Mrs. Hudson came up the stairs not two minutes later. "This just came for you, Mr. Holmes."

"Not another case," I groaned.

"Fear not, Watson," said Holmes as he read the telegraph. "It's just a reply from my brother. We are expected at the Diogenes at eight."

"For dinner, I hope."

"Of course," he replied.

I then understood why Holmes had forestalled my questions. He hated repeating himself, and I was pretty certain Mycroft and I had a great many questions in common for his brother and my friend.

We just had time to clean up and make ourselves presentable when Mrs. Hudson once again knocked on our door. "There's a cab here for you, Mr. Holmes."

"Thank you, dear lady. Please inform the driver we shall be down presently."

Twenty minutes later we were sitting in the Stranger's Room waiting for Mycroft to join us. A small table that featured place settings for three had been placed in the centre of the room. We hadn't long to wait as Mycroft lumbered in after about five minutes. He poured himself a whiskey from the sideboard and lowered his considerable bulk into a wing chair. "I have had quite the day," he told us.

I wasn't certain how to respond and waited to see what Holmes would say. However, at that moment, the door opened, and a young man wheeled in a trolley laden with dishes. "Once again, I took the liberty of ordering for everyone," Mycroft informed us after the waiter had left.

"Now, let me begin before you start, Sherlock. All afternoon and into the early evening, we've been inundated by reports of a mysterious explosion in the sky over Kent. In fact, we've had several people suggest that it might be Martians invading."

"Martians?" I said incredulously.

"Yes, apparently that H.G. Wells fellow has written a book. *War of the Worlds*, I believe it's called, in which Martians attempt to invade Earth. Utter rubbish. In addition to that I've had far more phone calls than I know what to do with. Although I do enjoy the convenience provided by the telephone, I simply can't abide it when it rings incessantly."

"Do tell?" inquired Holmes innocently.

"Well, I didn't ask you here to tell you about my day; however, I am desperate to hear about yours, so start from the beginning, Sherlock, and don't leave anything out."

Holmes then began a recitation of our adventures, skipping over the parts with which Mycroft was familiar. When he had finished, Mycroft looked at him and asked, "A dirigible with an engine attached. Have you considered the possibilities?"

"I have," replied my friend, "and I must say they give me cause to be uneasy."

Holmes then looked at me, and said, "Now it's your turn, old friend. I promised to answer all your questions."

I wasn't quite certain where to begin, so I asked the first of two questions that had been bothering me all day. "When we rounded the wall on the grounds of the lodge, I was taken aback by the sight of the dirigible. However, you said you expected such a thing. How on Earth could you have anticipated a dirigible in Kent?"

Holmes chuckled, "As I explained at the time, I thought they would need a machine of some sort to disseminate the spores. While I thought they might employ a balloon of some sort, my suspicions were confirmed only when we visited the dead sailmaker's shop."

"What could have possibly suggested a balloon at that point?"

"You may recall that in the shed that served as his workshop there were a number of trays on the floor filled with a white residue."

"Yes, I remember thinking it was some sort of special oil or paint that he applied to his sails to make them more durable – linseed oil perhaps."

"You are quite close, Watson. However, linseed oil is yellow. Had you examined them, you would have discovered that the residue was actually liquid rubber. Quince made the covering of the balloon – probably more than one – for them. I have no doubt the rest of the dirigible was made either in Germany or France, probably the latter, and imported into the country quite legally."

"Why not do the same with the covering?"

"I can only assume they wanted the covering to be new. Heat and age can help deteriorate both cloth and latex, and they didn't want the covering sitting around for any length of time before they used it.

"Also, you may remember the new windows Quince had installed in the shed. Liquid rubber gives off a strong odor which is caused by the chemicals involved in its production and curing. I'm sure Quince found it overpowering hence the sudden need for ventilation."

"That's all well and good, and I may be out of line here…"

Before I could finish my thought there was a knock on the door, and the same young man who had served dinner, entered and handed Mycroft a telegram. He read it, glanced at Holmes and, after the lad departed, said, "My men just discovered a second uninflated dirigible on an abandoned estate in Suffolk. They are continuing to look in the other areas you suggested."

"What were you about to ask, Watson?" inquired Holmes.

"When the dirigible exploded, you seemed to take it in stride. Did you also expect that, too?"

"In a very real sense," replied my friend, "I am responsible for the deaths of Edelman and Fritz although I must admit that I shan't be losing any sleep over it."

"How? What did you do?"

"You recall those crates marked for Edelman which we waylaid for a day?"

"Yes, there were big bottles of some liquid and sacks of something else."

"The liquid was both colourless and odourless."

"Yes, I remember wondering why he was shipping bottles of water – although I remember thinking, it was probably a ruse of some sort."

"No, there was no ruse. Those bottles contained sulfuric acid and the sacks contained lead filings. When you add lead to the acid…"

"You get hydrogen," I said cutting him off.

"Exactly. I tested both while you were gone just to be certain. Initially, I was tempted to add a base to the acid and neutralize it, but if Edelman should spot the change –

something I thought most likely – all our plans would be for naught."

"So what did you do?"

"I visited the local apothecary in Ashford and purchased a small amount of potash, which I added to one of the sacks. I then added some sugar to the filings in the other sack. If they hadn't mixed them, they might have survived. You must remember I did warn them that air travel was fraught with peril."

"So you did," I agreed. "But how could you have known it would be just Edelman and Fritz in the dirigible and not some innocent crew members as well?"

"Given the volume of chemicals we took off the train, I surmised that it had to be a relatively small dirigible and thus an even smaller gondola."

"So that was why you were desperate to secure Miss Adler's freedom?"

"Yes, I couldn't be certain my plan would work, but I had every expectation they would just throw the filings into the acid willy-nilly in an attempt to get as high as possible as quickly as possible and as far away as the wind and their engine would carry them."

"Could it have played out any differently? I would have preferred to see both men standing in the dock."

"I'm not certain it could have," replied Holmes. "As I said, although they posed a grave threat, they hadn't broken any laws – at least none that we could prove that would hold up in court."

"And are you pleased with the way things turned out?"

He paused thoughtfully and then said, "Pleased, no. No man's death pleases me. Edelman was brilliant, but he decided to follow the wrong path. In the end, as you know, I'd rather play tricks with the English law than my conscience. Edelman was an evil man who would have made millions suffer and whose actions might have resulted in the deaths of untold thousands perhaps millions."

"Millions?" I asked.

"Historians believe between 1 and 3 million people died as a result of the Irish potato famine. Some maintain as many as 100,000 perished on the coffin ships. Can you imagine the number who might have lost their lives trying to flee England?" Holmes then lapsed into silence.

Mycroft had remained quiet while my friend explained his actions. Finally he said, "It is difficult to muster any sympathy for the passing of those men and the threat they posed.

"However, I will say within the confines of this room, that while your government is grateful, it is unfortunate, but your" – and here he hesitated as he searched for just the right word – "work can never be acknowledged." Then he glanced at me and said, "I trust you take my meaning, Doctor."

All I could do was nod in agreement.

Chapter Seventeen

The next evening at half seven, as agreed, I met Miss Adler, Dr. Roberts and Lieutenant Tagliamonti at Rules. I made excuses for Holmes, saying he had immediately become involved in another case of some importance.

We discussed all we had shared, and they assailed me with questions throughout the evening. I answered as discreetly as I might, always being careful never to give too much away.

Tagliamonti was leaving the next morning for Italy. He planned to travel to Dover and then through France by rail until he had made his way to Milan. Dr. Roberts was all too ready to return to his research. "Although I appreciated the adventure, I can't say that I totally enjoyed it," he remarked.

Miss Adler's plans were less certain. She intended to remain in London for a few more days and was undecided about visiting Ireland or returning to the United States. When we had bid each other farewell outside the restaurant, she turned to me and said, "If it is at all possible, I should very much like to see Mr. Holmes one more time before I depart. Please see if that can be arranged. You can contact me at the Langham. I never did give up my room."

When I returned home, I found Holmes sitting in front of the fire enjoying a pipe. I poured us both a brandy, and after I had settled myself, I told him all about the dinner and the various bits of news that he had missed. Finally, I reached the point where I said Miss Adler had requested to see him once more before leaving London.

"To what end?" he asked. "She played her part, and she played it bravely and well. I'm not certain anything else need be said."

"It would be a kindness, Holmes. After all, it was through her seeking justice for her sister that you became involved in the case. So one might argue that in a very indirect way, it was she who saved the Empire."

Holmes peered up at me with a quizzical look on his face. Then his features relaxed, and he grinned. "When you put it that way, Watson, how can I refuse? It would be akin to turning down a request from Joan of Arc."

"Excellent! I shall invite her to lunch or would you prefer supper?"

"Supper, I think, that will give everyone, including Mrs. Hudson, a bit more time to prepare.

Now, I smiled, and before he could change his mind, I composed a quick note and hurried downstairs and left it where the boy in buttons would find it first thing in the morning. I also penned a second note informing Mrs. Hudson that we would have a very special guest for dinner at seven. I knew that was all she needed to hear in order to unleash her culinary skills. As I walked back up the stairs, I thought to myself, "If nothing, else, we'll eat well tomorrow night."

The next morning I woke to discover that it was a gloriously sunny day. Holmes was absent for breakfast, so I dined alone. As I descended the stairs on my way to the hospital, the page informed me he had delivered the note and received a response, whereupon he handed me an envelope, which contained a brief reply.

Looking forward to this evening. Thank you!

As I was about to open the door, Mrs. Hudson came bustling in laden with purchases and promptly informed me that she would be preparing a joint of beef along with seasonal vegetables for dinner and her specialty, a bread-and-butter pudding, for dessert.

The day flew by, and I was looking forward to seeing how Holmes would react to an evening with the sister of *the woman* in a fairly intimate setting.

As you might expect, Miss Adler arrived promptly at seven. I opened the door to discover a vision of loveliness. She looked stunning in an outfit of midnight blue that showed off her fair skin, and once again I saw that face a man might die for. She swept across the room and curtseyed in front of Holmes, who bowed deeply.

"It is a pleasure to see you again, madame, and this time under rather more pleasant circumstances."

After drinks, we settled down to dinner. The evening, at least for me, was something of a dichotomy. There were moments of pleasant, perhaps even inspired, conversation that were offset by prolonged silences. Still, I must admit that such stretches seemed more natural than awkward.

After we had finished dessert and Mrs. Hudson was clearing away the remnants, Miss Adler complimented our landlady on both the presentation of the meal and her culinary skill. After Mrs. Hudson, who was positively glowing in the wake of our visitor's comments, had departed, Holmes observed, "I think you shall never want for sustenance as long as Mrs. Hudson has access to a kitchen."

After we had settled into our chairs with brandy and cigarettes, Miss Adler said, "I wanted to thank you personally, Mr. Holmes, and you too, Dr. Watson, for your efforts to bring that fiend, Edelman, to justice. I shall sleep better knowing my sister and Godfrey have been avenged."

Holmes, never comfortable in such situations, smiled and said, "It was the least I could do. Although your sister and I met under rather adverse circumstances, I very much admired her."

"And she you, Mr. Holmes."

After a pause, she sighed and said, "I miss her terribly." I thought I detected the trace of a tear as she dabbed at her eyes.

"You are very much like her," observed my friend. "Both physically and in that inner steel that refuses to yield to pressure."

I could see that she was touched as she expressed her appreciation for his compliment.

With that, Holmes rose to his feet and said, "I have something for you." He then went to his desk opened the top drawer and returned with a small wooden frame with which I was quite familiar. Years ago, Holmes had placed the photo which he had requested from the King of Bohemia in lieu of payment for his work in averting a scandal involving His Majesty, in that frame, and he kept the frame is his top drawer. It was a photograph of Irene Adler in evening dress, and she looked positively radiant.

"I have long treasured this photograph of your sister, and now I would like you to have it."

"Oh, I couldn't Mr. Holmes. It is a keepsake – something to remember her by."

"Believe me, madame," said Holmes as he fingered the gold sovereign on his watch chain, "I have something by which I will always remember her. Moreover, I received it on what I believe was one of the happiest days of her life. Please take this, it would mean a great deal to me."

We then enjoyed another brandy, and as it was growing late, Miss Adler said, "I really must be on my way. I have a train to catch in the morning. Thank you for everything, Mr. Holmes and Dr. Watson, and do give my regards to Mrs. Hudson once more in the morning."

Holmes and I escorted her to the door and descended the stairs with her. I ran ahead to hail a cab for her and watched as she took her seat in a rather handsome landau. As the cab started down the street, it suddenly slowed, and Miss Adler leaned her head out the window and said, "Good night, Dr. Watson." After a brief pause, she added, "Good night, Mr. Sherlock Holmes."

The End

Epilogue

As had been the case with her sister, Irene Adler, we never did encounter Miss Serena Adler again.

As you might expect, Holmes quickly moved on to his next case which involved a man who, having bid his wife and young daughter good-bye, went to work in the City one Tuesday morning and returned home that evening to discover an entirely different family – one with three children, all boys – now residing in his house. Moreover, when questioned by the police, the neighbors all swore to the fact that the "new" family he had encountered had been living in the house for more than a decade. It proved to be one of the strangest cases of Holmes's long and storied career. However, that is a tale for another day.

As he continued to work, taking cases from scullery maids to stole-draped duchesses, Holmes encountered any number of attractive, intelligent women over the course of his career, but despite their many advantages, to him they were all merely clients.

I knew Holmes valued my company, but as is quite obvious from my observations over the years, he was also quite content to keep his own counsel. While getting him to opine on such subjects as crime and his own unique niche as a consulting detective was remarkably easy, any attempt to elicit his feelings about women and other such matters was akin to taking on one of the labours of Hercules.

However, having twice been exposed to charms of women named Adler, Holmes now had a broader scale by which to judge and measure all others of their sex. As you might expect, few if any measured up. And if they had cleared that high bar, he never spoke about them – at least to me anyway.

Despite the passage of years and the dawn of a new century, things went on pretty much as they always had at 221B.

Having survived that most compelling of interruptions, we slipped back into our ways of the tobacco in the Persian slipper, cigars in the coal scuttle and correspondence affixed to the mantel with a jackknife – and a never-ending parade of supplicants from all walks of life knocking at our door.

Holmes seldom if ever mentioned either Irene or Serena Adler, but on those rare occasions when he did, he always referred to them with the utmost respect as either *the woman* or *the other woman*. You can be certain I always knew exactly about whom he was speaking.

– Dr. John Watson

11 December, 1902

Author's Notes

While much of this book is a work of fiction, some of the people named herein actually did exist. Worthington G. Smith was an accomplished botanist and illustrator, and he really did discover the *fusarium* wheat blight which plays such a crucial role in this story. Also, all the pioneering balloonists mentioned near the end existed; it's unfortunate we don't know more about them.

As you might have suspected, many of the places mentioned can still be seen today. For example, Edelman's residence at 4 Carlton House Terrace did serve as the German embassy to London until the embassy was moved to 9 Carlton House Terrace.

The trio of tobacco shops named by Bradley – Robert Lewis on St. James Street, Fribourg & Treyer at 34 Haymarket, and Inderwicks in Wardour Street, Soho, were three of the preeminent tobacconists serving London in the Victorian era.

The Electrical Power Storage Co., Ltd., really did display a sign proclaiming "Storage Battery Makers by Warrant to His Majesty The King." And in 1902, it was located on the Isle of Dogs.

Should you ever find yourself visiting Canterbury, you can stop by The Three Mariners, but there is no public house called The Ewe and Cry, nor is there an estate by the name of Red Fox Lodge. Also, don't bother looking for The Wailing Siren in Ashford.

Finally, with regard to places, although there is a Curley's Trout Fishery located not too far from Manchester,

I should not look for a nearby farm that suffered from a failed wheat crop.

It is also worth noting Thomas Edison did invent an electric heater in 1883, just a few short years after he had designed the light bulb.

Last but not least I should also mention when Holmes holds forth on ballooning, that too is based upon historical records, including the fairly recent invention – at that time – of the dirigible.

Acknowledgments

After a decade of producing novels and other pieces, I still believe writing, at least as I practice it, is a lonely task. I'm in awe of those people who can sit down and collaborate and produce a book together. As I've mentioned in the past, when I get stuck, I have no "Lifelines." I can't "Phone a Friend" and ask for a denouement nor can I "Buy a Villain." Over the years, I've gotten into the habit of writing late at night when everyone else is in bed and the house is still. However, it has been made somewhat less onerous by the encouragement and patience of friends and family members, especially my wife, who have supported and cheered me on in my endeavors.

The first person I need to thank is my wife, Grace. I wouldn't be a writer without her encouragement, patience, and honest criticism. I am the luckiest man alive.

I should also be terribly remiss if I failed to thank my publisher, Steve Emecz, who continues to make the process painless and who also is a great source of encouragement. I am blessed to have my covers designed by the enormously talented Brian Belanger, whose skill in that area is unmatched. To have such talented friends is a blessing indeed.

No book is complete without a solid line edit, and Deborah Annakin Peters continues to provide that as well as a number of invaluable suggestions all of which have improved my books immeasurably. She also makes certain that my Britishisms are correct (I still can't believe they don't say gotten.) and that no Americanisms are allowed to creep in. My works are so much better because of her diligence and care.

I also owe a considerable debt to Dr. Robert Katz, a good friend, who remains the finest Sherlockian I know. He has continued to encourage me and is kind enough to read my efforts with an eye toward accuracy – both with regard to the Canon, and perhaps more importantly, to common sense.

To my brother, Edward; and my sister, Arlene; who continue to believe in me even when I am constantly doubting myself.

I owe a special debt to many of my former students – a number of whom have somehow found their way onto my pages – who have read and enjoyed my books and offered kind words of support. You know who you are, and I can't thank you enough.

A very special thank you to Chet Boles, Steven Smith, Marianne Pittorino, Joe Wojno, and Maureen Fairlie; your continued support is greatly appreciated.

Finally, to all those, and there are far too many to name, whose support for my earlier efforts has made me see just what a wonderful life I have and what great people I am surrounded by, a sincere thank you.

To say that I am in the debt of all those mentioned here doesn't even begin to scratch the surface of my gratitude.

Finally, once again, if there are errors in this book – and I'm pretty sure there are – the only person responsible for them is me.

About the author

Richard T. Ryan is a native New Yorker, having been born and raised on Staten Island. He majored in English literature at St. Peter's College (now St. Peter's University) in Jersey City and pursued his graduate studies, concentrating on medieval literature, at the University of Notre Dame in Indiana.

After teaching high school and college for more than a decade, he joined the staff of the Staten Island Advance newspaper. He worked there for nearly 30 years, rising through the ranks to become the news editor.

When he retired in 2016, he held the position of publications manager for that paper although he still prefers the title, news editor.

In addition to his first novel, "The Vatican Cameos: A Sherlock Holmes Adventure," he has written "The Stone of Destiny," "The Druid of Death," "The Merchant of Menace," "Through a Glass Starkly," "Three May Keep a Secret," "The Poisoned Pawn," "The Devil's Disciples" and "The Traitorous Templar" – all of which feature Holmes and Watson. To date, seven of his novels have been published in Italian by Mondadori, and *The Vatican Cameos* has been released in Spanish by La de Grandes Detalles .

Other published works include *B Is for Baker Street: My First Sherlock Holmes Book*, which he wrote for his grandchildren, Riley Grace, Henry Robert and Brody Edward.

He has also penned three trivia books, including *The Official Sherlock Holmes Trivia Book.*

Wearing a different hat, he serves as the editor for the *Year in Mystery* series for Belanger Books, which attempts to fill in the voids in the Sherlockian Canon. The first eight books, 1881 through 1888, are available and the ninth and tenth volumes are due out later this year. Also for Belanger Books, he has co-edited *Writing Holmes,* a collection of essays on why and how people write about the world's Greatest Detective; and *Reading Holmes* with *Seeing Holmes,* due out later at some point in the future. He also served as editor for *No Holidays for Holmes,* a collection of short stories, and is hoping to compile a second volume someday.

In a slightly different medium, he can also boast at having had *Deadly Relations,* a mystery-thriller he penned produced off-Broadway on two separate occasions at the Playwrights Horizons Theatre.

And if that weren't enough, he is the very proud father of two children, Dr. Kaitlin Ryan-Smith and Michael Ryan, and the incredibly proud grandfather of the aforementioned Riley Grace and Henry Robert as well as Brody Edward, the newest member of the Ryan clan.

He has been married for 47 years to his wife, Grace, and continues to marvel at her incredible patience in putting up with him and his computer illiteracy.

At the moment, he is undecided about what his next project will be. Although he is considering editing another of the unpublished manuscripts from Dr. Watson's tin dispatch box.

Keep reading for an excerpt from Richard T. Ryan's
next book:

The Apache Assassin

(A working title)

Chapter One

I returned home one evening in late 1904; November, I believe it was, to discover a telegram waiting for me on my kitchen table. I looked at it, and I must admit a slight thrill ran up my spine.

Although almost everyone had access to a telephone at that point, including my dear friend, Sherlock Holmes, I knew that his preferred means of communication was by wire.

Since he had retired to the Sussex Downs a year earlier to tend to his bees, I had seen him but twice. Although we corresponded, it was irregular at best. To say I missed him would be an understatement.

I had settled into the life of an aging physician, but I must admit that I missed those days when Holmes would proclaim, "The game is afoot!" and we'd set off on one of our adventures.

While some men are able to wear their years like a well-tailored suit; sadly, I am not one of them. Although I was now more than two score and ten, I thought I carried my years well, and I generally felt in fine fettle. Truth be told, I had grown weary of the routine of a physician and longed for those days when Holmes and I, like a pair of knights errant, would set out to vanquish evil in all its manifestations.

Tentatively I picked up the telegram and ripped it open. As I read the few words, I will be the first to admit that my heart leaped with excitement.

Come at once if convenient.
If inconvenient, come all the same!

SH – 221B

Holmes had first used an identical summons just a year earlier during one of our final investigations, a case which has yet to be published. It had proven to be an invitation to one of our more bizarre adventures, and truth be told, I was secretly hoping that this latest summons might provide us with an equally challenging task.

At this point, I should say there is a great deal of truth in the old axiom: Be careful what you wish for.

However, I was so thrilled to be invited to join the hunt that the thought of tragedy never even crossed my mind.

I immediately left my home and hailed a cab. When I gave the driver the address, he cast a knowing look my way. When I alighted from the hansom some twenty minutes later, I felt a mix of excitement and trepidation. I wondered if I still had the mettle to keep up with Holmes, and there was always that slight undercurrent of fear that presaged learning exactly what we might be getting ourselves involved in.

Holmes had kept the rooms in Baker Street so that he might have a familiar refuge on those rare occasions when he found it necessary to return to London. I wasn't certain if he had purchased the building from Mrs. Hudson – he certainly had the financial wherewiithal to do so – or if he were still a tenant. At any rate, when I rang the bell my former landlady answered. "Oh, Doctor Watson, it's so good to see you, and you are looking well. Mr. Holmes arrived yesterday morning – unannounced, I might add. It's taken me the better part of yesterday and today to set things right. Of course, the dust and such never bothered Mr. Holmes, but I take pride in keeping a neat and orderly house."

"Of course you do, dear lady, and while Mr. Holmes may not always express his appreciation, rest assured that your efforts do not go unnoticed."

Having smoothed over that bit of troubled water to the best of my ability, I climbed the steps and knocked on the door of my old flat. From within, I heard Holmes bellow, "Watson, do come in."

I entered to find my friend wearing his mouse-brown dressing gown and sitting at his chemistry table examining something – I couldn't quite see what it was – with his lens. As soon I had crossed the threshold, he put down his glass and strode across the room to greet me.

"You are looking fit as a fiddle, old friend, and your practice is thriving, I see. Also, you have a new housekeeper. Although she appears quite competent, she doesn't quite measure up to your previous one. Still, she may grow into the position. Give her time, old friend."

After all our years together I was used to Holmes making such proclamations, and I was always a little unnerved at his uncanny accuracy. "Obviously, my attire would certainly give some indication as to the state of my practice."

"Indeed, I don't think I have ever seen you in a bespoke suit before. Savile Row? Henry Poole and Co., I should think. The high gorge line is a dead give-away."

"You haven't lost your touch, old friend. However, I am more impressed with your deductions about my new housekeeper."

"Simplicity, itself!" He exclaimed. "Never a slave to fashion, you had no idea what a pocket square was until you wed Mary. Thereafter, you were never without a crisply starched two-point fold in your breast pocket. After your wife passed, your housekeeper, Abagail, continued the practice. However today I see you sporting a simple one-point fold that is both limp and a bit bedraggled in your pocket – I trust the chain is obvious."

"Marvelous, Holmes!" I exclaimed. "I must admit that such trifles as pocket squares have never commanded my attention."

"Obviously," he replied, "and yet how often have I told you there is nothing so important as trifles."

At that we both laughed, and Holmes said, "Sherry?"

I agreed and after he had poured the drinks we settled into our chairs – just like old times.

"So what is so important that you have given up your beekeeping for the present and issued me a summons that seemed more like a command than an invitation?

"Obviously, you knew the wording would pique my interest – just as it did a year ago."

"Guilty as charged," he admitted. "Actually, I've left my bees in the care of Sorenson, my neighbor. A week ago I was summoned to France whence I have just returned. It's a rather nasty business, and one that I should like to have my old friend by my side as I dig into it."

"Do tell," I urged him.

"Have you ever heard of the Apaches?"

"Of course! I know something about the tribe as well as some of their leaders – Geronimo, Cochise and Victorio, to name just a few."

Holmes chuckled, "I suppose I should have sad *Les Apaches* – and not the artistic group founded by Ravel."

"Is there another such group with that name?"

"Indeed, there is. They are the scourge of Paris – a violent street gang currently plaguing that fair city and terrorising its residents. If reports are to be believed, they number some 30,000 members while the Paris police force has only 8,000 men."

"My word!"

"I'm sure the numbers are exaggerated, but their ruthlessness is not. In fact, it is their savagery that has earned them the sobriquet which explicitly ties them to the American Indian tribe."

"Surely, they are not scalping people?"

"Actually, the American Apaches seldom if ever scalped anyone. That's a myth that somehow has gained currency."

"Do tell."

"No, these Apaches prefer a tactic known as the *coup du Père François,* which may be loosely translated as 'The Shot of Father Francis.' After stalking their victim, several members of the gang attack and while one garrotes the victim from behind and carries him piggyback so as to prevent struggling another searches through the victim's pockets for any valuables, while a third stands guard as lookout. Although the intent is usually only to incapacitate their victim, a number of deaths from strangulation have occurred."

"Holmes, that is simply incredible."

"I agree wholeheartedly. Now I am certain you recall Huret, the Boulevard assassin? I believe you mentioned him in one of your tales."

"Of course, it was late in '94, after your miraculous resurrection. As I recall, you went to Paris where you tracked and finally arrested that blackguard. If I remember correctly, your efforts earned you an autographed letter of thanks from the French President and you were presented with the Order of the Legion of Honour."

"Indeed," he said dismissively. "However, what I did not know at the time was that Huret had a protege. He had taken a student under his wing, if you will, and was serving as a mentor of sorts, imparting all the tricks of the trade to his disciple."

"But that was a decade ago. What have the events of 1894 to do with today?"

"Huret died in prison a few days ago. Before his death, he implored the authorities to bring me to his bedside. 'Consider it the last wish of a dying man,' he told them. He also implied to the French authorities that it was a matter of some urgency. Our old friend Francois Bencolin of the Surete reached out to me. As there was nothing pressing, I made the trip to France, wondering whether I'd be meeting a repentant Huret or one who would revile me with curses for having had him imprisoned."

"Where was he being held?"

"He was being detained in the Fontevraud Penitentiary, about 130 miles south of Paris in the Loire Valley. It's a fascinating place, Watson, with strong ties to English history, but I digress."

"And when you got there, which Huret did you find?"

"Neither, actually," replied Holmes. "While he certainly didn't express remorse for anything he had done, neither was he the ranting and raving lunatic I had feared. Rather he exhibited a certain calm acceptance of his impending fate, and that may have been the most chilling aspect of entire meeting.

"He was chained to his bed, and asked the guard if we might be alone for a moment. The guard acquiesced and stepped into the corridor. Once he had departed, Huret look at me and then whispered, 'I have longed for this moment for years, Holmes. I have cancer and at most a few weeks perhaps days left to live. I just want you to know that my enmity for you knows no bounds. I have paid for my crimes, but you will pay – and pay dearly – for what you have done to me. I give you fair warning, Holmes. From this day forward your life could be forfeit at any moment.'

"He was so dispassionate in his pronouncement that I found his words all the more chilling. 'I have friends, Holmes, many, many friends. I also have one particularly special friend, *la prunelle de mes yeux, mon joyah de la couronne.*'

"The apple of my eye, my crown jewel," he called this person. 'They will come for you, Holmes, and just like my imprisonment here, your death will long and unpleasant.'"

"My word, Holmes, what an extraordinary tale!"

"It gets even more bizarre, my friend. I returned to Paris where I spoke with Bencolin. I asked if they kept records of all who had visited Huret in prison. I was informed they did. In fact, there were two copies – one at Fontevraud Penitentiary and a second one in Paris.

"However, when he went to get the list of those who had visited Huret, he discovered that the pages had been carefully removed from the book. And when he phoned the prison, he discovered that Huret's book was missing."

"Had to be one of the guards at the prison," I said.

"And a corrupt gendarme in Paris?" asked Holmes. "Yes, those were my thoughts exactly. The next day I took a train back to the prison only to discover that Huret had died that morning."

"Dead men tell no tales."

"Nor can they be questioned. I returned to Paris and caught a train to Calais. I was trying to decide if they were the threats of a bitter man seeking some small sense of revenge by making me worry about ghosts, or if they had merit."

"And what did you decide?"

Holding up his right arm, Holmes allowed the sleeve of his dressing gown to fall, and I saw that his forearm, from two inches above the wrist to his elbow, was heavily bandaged.

"After an encounter with an Apache as the boat docked in Dover, I'm inclined to think his words were anything but idle threats."